At Worl

Levi F. Fox

Bluesource And Friends

This book is brought to you by Bluesource And Friends, a happy book publishing company.

Our motto is **"Happiness Within Pages"**
We promise to deliver amazing value to readers with our books.
We also appreciate honest book reviews from our readers.

Connect with us on our Facebook page www.facebook.com/bluesourceandfriends and stay tuned to our latest book promotions and free giveaways.

Don't forget to claim your FREE books!

Brain Teasers:
https://tinyurl.com/karenbrainteasers
Harry Potter Trivia:
https://tinyurl.com/wizardworldtrivia
Sherlock Puzzle Book (Volume 2)
https://tinyurl.com/Sherlockpuzzlebook2

Also check out our best seller books

"67 Lateral Thinking Puzzles"
https://tinyurl.com/thinkingandriddles

"Rookstorm Online Saga"
https://tinyurl.com/rookstorm

At World's End

Table of Contents

Description

Zac knows very well that there is more to the world than meets his eye, and so when his father introduces him to a new magical world, his experiences change completely. He does some detective work by finding out what is going on with the invisible magical forces that control the world. However, he gets caught up in a war that is sweeping through their country, and his father removes him from the situation in the most peculiar way. Zac is sent to live with some of his relatives, but what he does not realize is that he is traveling to the end of the world. Utterly bewildered that there is life in other regions of the world that are completely unknown to the rest of the masses, Zac finds it hard to adjust to the cold weather and all the secrecy that seems to exist where he has been sent. He meets a new friend, but he also gets to witness a lot of supernatural instances that leave him puzzled and even with more questions than before. His detective work leads him to discover truths that he would rather have avoided. He ends up concluding his sleuthing in utter surprise and shock.

PROLOGUE

The Kingdom of the Gods.

Dear People of the Universe,

<u>RE: LET THE TRUTH NEVER BE REVEALED</u>

It has come to my knowledge that some of you are sharing sensitive and forbidden knowledge with the people living on earth.

I want to take this opportunity to express my displeasure and disgust with any individual found communicating directly with human beings.

We all have a responsibility for being moral and outstanding beings. We are different from human beings, and we shall remain different despite their importance since being created. With that being said,

there will be punishments awaiting those found

collaborating with human beings.

The truth shall not be revealed.

X

**The Kingdom of
The Gods**

At World's End

I could not fathom the contents of the letter, but I knew something dangerous was about to happen to the world. I would have to engage in some detective work in order to understand exactly what I was getting myself into.

Most people do not believe in magic; give me a moment to laugh.

After all, everything about us *is* magic. What do we know about the gods who brought us here, and how sure can we be that they mind our best interests? There is nothing more terrifying than not knowing the truth.

I would rather face ten people attacking me and know exactly what I am getting into. Magic is everything—it is the very foundation of Creation. However, magic itself can be defined in several ways.

I am always curious as to what will happen once the truth is universally known. So many people live blindly that they simply cannot accept a fact when it happens. For instance, the world we live in is all magic—right from its start to the point that we have reached.

However, most people do not realize this—and worse yet, they try to fight the obvious. The gods are making plans for us, and I would like to know, more than anything, what those plans are. I have no intention of getting caught by surprise.

At World's End

There is an inevitable conflict coming that will affect every single human being as well as every civilization on earth. I have come to realize that there are several different types of gods, and the key is in identifying the most important and strongest of them all.

What can we say about the gods, anyway? The only evidence we have of their existence is the magic that is on display in this world. However, is their magic that powerful when you leave this world? And who is the most powerful of the gods?

I have always been curious about the world around me, but my parents have never allowed me to do much research about it. Every time I mention about "gods" in the house, my mother gets a fit, while my father gives me a very disapproving glance.

At World's End

I want to know everything; I am not leaving this world without fining the truth about the people who truly control everything. I want to know what inspires them to make the decisions they do, and I also want to know if human beings truly are in control.

It is very important to me to know where we are heading, and thus also where we have come from. Most people simply ignore this fact because they are too fearful of questioning the gods, but the question is: Are we responding to the right gods?

I looked at the letter once again then got out of bed—my head spinning and slight dizziness taking over my body. It was a cold London winter, and I was hoping it would get a little warm. I trudged to the bathroom—my mind filled with hundreds of questions.

Detective work was upon me. I would have to find out where the letter came from and the severity of the threat that human beings face—but it was work I would have to do all by myself because the DCI at my office simply did not believe in supernatural tales.

According to them, there are much bigger things to be chasing after. Crime levels in Britain are at an all-time high–more youth are turning to drugs and violence, and there has been an increased number of violent attacks against politicians.

However, for me, I felt that the scale of the threat we were facing was much bigger. This was the advantage of being raised in a no-nonsense family because it allowed me to discover so much about the world as a young person.

Once I was back in bed, I went through the letter once more, surprised that nobody took the threat we were facing with the seriousness it deserved. I had once soared in the sky, so high up, and that was the day my detective life changed completely.

None of my colleagues at work seemed to appreciate the manner in which I had changed my life; there was so much to be wary about that I realized ordinary detective work did not make any sense at all.

This was because we are surrounded by so many entities to the point that it is impossible to understand the threats truly facing humanity. I came to realize that the threats facing humanity are much more serious than we would like to believe.

I was dreaming when I found myself somewhere high above the clouds. It was a cold day, and there was a thick cloud cover, completely inhibiting my vision. The fluffiness of the clouds seemed like something tangible, but the higher I went, the more I realized that I was never going to be able to touch them.

When I was high enough, I started panicking—and despite the cold, a slight sweat started dripping down my visage. I was not quite sure what I was doing so high up in the sky, let alone being aware that I was in a dream.

At World's End

However, what appeared to be a small settlement suddenly came into view, and the clouds that were passing beneath my feet suddenly solidified, and it was as though I was standing on bare ground.

There were old-fashioned buildings right before me, high up in the clouds. They looked like ancient Buddhist settlements, and there was even a large statue of what must have been one of the gods.

The place looked magical because everywhere was as white as the fluffy clouds. I started asking myself what I was doing there, knowing all too well that I was in another world. However I was not scared at all, and my detective instincts started kicking in.

At World's End

I took timid baby steps across the clouds, worried that maybe I would fall through the fluffy clouds—but I was surprised that the clouds were as solid and hard as the ground on Earth was. There were strange shadows playing about everywhere, and I started wondering how I had discovered this strange world right above our world.

I approached one of the monastery-looking buildings, then realized it was an actual monastery. It was a genuine place of worship once I had gotten through the doors, but what really caught my eye were the numerous statues decorating the large room.

"Hello?" I called out. "Hello? Anybody here?"

At World's End

My voice echoed off the walls; it was confirmation that I was all alone. It was time for some sleuthing. I needed to find out everything about this strange new place I had discovered. I was hoping to arm myself with enough information about the gods.

And that is when I noticed that there was an intimidating presence right behind me. I turned around instantly, realizing that I had walked in far enough into the monastery. The sight that met me was truly shocking.

There was a large, black beast with horns coming out of its partially-visible head staring down at me with beetroot-red eyes. It was very large—its head almost touching the ceiling. Its entire body was furry, just like a bear, and it had large claws both on its hands and feet.

My mouth swung wide open—I wanted to scream in shock, but only air came out of my mouth. The creature was staring at me patiently, breathing hard, with its whole body heaving in a tremendous motion.

Its breathing was so strange that it appeared as though steam was coming out from its mouth and nose. It just stood there, staring hard at me as I remained rooted to the spot. There was nowhere for me to run, and there was nothing I could do to defend myself in that instance.

The creature was so big that I was certain that if I turned around and started running within the monastery, it would simply swing its large claws and put an end to my tomfoolery.

Where had it come from? I had not seen it.

But I figured that if there were going to be buildings in the Heavens, something must be responsible for their construction.

"Who are you?" The words finally managed to escape my mouth. But I was also breathing hard from nervousness, and I was wondering what was about to happen to me.

The creature then lifted its hands into the air, and I was sure that I was about to be struck. I was going to die in my own dream—die such a senseless death

At World's End

without even realizing what was going on. I closed my
eyes, waiting for the fatal clubbing blow.

But when I opened my eyes, I was suddenly back
down on Earth—in the middle of Trafalgar Street, to
be precise. I looked around the bustling place and
heaved a sigh of relief.

Up to this day, I have never understood what that
dream was all about.

Chapter 1

When Zac was first informed that he would have to

go on holiday and visit his grandparents outside of

the kingdom, he was particularly upset by this

proposition.

"I have a life, you know," he argued one night when

his father had come back from work.

"For once," said his father, trotting through the front

door of their bungalow and slamming it shut with a

sigh of relief, "listen to me."

Zac was already furious that he would have to be

separated from his friends. He had spent the entire

summer working for one of his father's friends, and

he was looking forward to finishing the rest of the holiday relaxing around familiar faces.

"There's going to be a war," said Zac's father, taking a seat in their small, miniature sitting room.

Zac did not particularly like their house—it was small, located next to a large mountain in the biggest forest on the island. They did not have many neighbors, but Zac always preferred being outside than being cramped in the small house.

However, the proposition from his father for him to visit his grandparents was going to be worse. He had never met them, and he had no idea where they lived.

"I don't feel comfortable going to live with a bunch of people I don't even know," said Zac.

At World's End

His father, who had now sprawled on the couch and had a newspaper close to his face, was in no mood for an argument.

"They're your grandparents, Zac," said his father. "You should not feel uncomfortable around them."

"What do you mean there's going to be a war?" Zac queried.

"Well," said Zac's father, shoving aside the newspaper which fell in a heap on the carpeted floor. "The King has refused to accept any kind of deal with the Egyptians, and so he has condemned the entire kingdom to war."

Zac's eyes bulged. "The Egyptians?"

At World's End

His father nodded. "Yes. We know little about them, but what we do know is that they control that other side of the world."

Zac remained speechless for a moment.

"That's why I need you to travel to your grandparents," Zac's father continued, "I need to ensure that you are safe."

"What about the rest of you?" asked Zac.

"We'll support our King and go to war to defend our country," said his father. "The situation has already deteriorated, and it has become unsafe for you to be here."

"What about Mom?" Zac asked.

He had not seen his mother for the last three years, although he always remained hopeful of seeing her again.

"There's probably nobody in the entire kingdom who's safer than your mother at this moment," said Zac's father.

"To be honest, Dad," said Zac, taking a seat next to his father, "I don't want to leave. I want to stay here and fight. Why do you insist on having me leave?"

Zac's father sighed loudly. He got up to his feet, almost hitting his head on the low ceiling. He proceeded to trod into the kitchen. Zac followed in tow.

At World's End

His father placed a kettle over the cooker and lit it, taking a cigarette from a cupboard directly above the sink and lighting it with the cooker's fire. The kitchen was suddenly filled with a rush of a smooth tobacco scent that made Zac's eyes water.

"You're a very important person, you know?" said Zac's father, touching his son's dark hair and ruffling it a little. "You and the rest of your age-mates are the future of this kingdom, after all. If we don't take care of you at this moment, the kingdom will eventually disappear."

"I won't die, Dad," said Zac, "I promise. Just let me stay here with you and fight."

At World's End

Zac's father smiled. He let out a large drag from his cigarette, setting it on the kitchen counter and kneeling on the kitchen floor to meet his son's frustrated eyes.

"Listen to me, Zac," said his father, the only way I can protect you is by sending you somewhere where you'll be safe. There are some things about our kingdom that you don't know, and until you're old enough, you will just have to listen to me."

"What is it, Dad? Just tell me."

Zac's father smiled again and got back to his feet. He took the cigarette off the kitchen counter and placed it in his mouth, taking another deep drag.

"Well, I suppose you're old enough."

At World's End

"Tell me, Dad."

Zac's father seemed to shrug to himself, and then he started speaking slowly after taking another drag of his cigarette.

"I suppose you've figured that your King is very much a superstitious man."

Zac shrugged.

"Well," his father continued, "this war is probably the greatest threat the kingdom has faced since it was founded a thousand years ago. A large army of heathens will descend on our beautiful kingdom, and the chance of success looks bleak."

At World's End

Zac frowned. "Why don't you come with me, then, Dad? If it's an unwinnable war, you should save yourself and Mom while you still can."

Zac's father smiled. "I hope it was that easy."

"It is easy!" Zac insisted. "Let's travel together, then."

"What I haven't told you yet is the strategy that the King is using to win this war."

Zac looked at his father. "There is hope for winning this war, then? That's surprising."

The cooker behind them let out a steaming noise, and Zac's father put out the fire. He proceeded to remove cups from the top shelf in the room and poured in a concoction of sugar, milk powder, and drinking chocolate. The cigarette was still burning seamlessly between his darkened lips.

"What are you not telling me, Dad?"

Zac's father sighed, putting the cigarette down on the kitchen counter.

"The King has gathered magicians from across the country and is killing all boys less than eighteen years of age in the kingdom as a sacrifice to the gods to grant us victory."

Chapter 2

The Kingdom of Atlantis was in a mess. Everybody was scrambling about trying to prepare the kingdom for war, and there were almost no little boys in sight.

Zac was wearing a heavily hooded jacket that was black in color and meant for the snow. His father had told him the previous night that he will need it for his journey. They were walking through the main town to his father's friend's house.

"How am I going to travel?" Zac had asked his father. "The King's guards are everywhere. How will I leave? I haven't even said goodbye to my friends."

Zac cast a warring look at his son. "That's if your friends are still alive."

At World's End

Zac's eyes widened. "James, Cathy and John."

"I need you to stay strong, son."

They turned out from the main street of the town that was crowded with people rushing everywhere, and they branched off to a small alley where a large mahogany door stood at the end of the path. When they reached it, Zac's father knocked twice, lightly.

In a matter of a second, the door opened eerily by itself, creaking loudly as it allowed flashes of light to invade the darkness within. A very thick, white smoke whiffed from the darkness and formed a cloud above the two visitors who stood motionlessly on the doorway.

"It's me, Dolores," said Zac's father, speaking up to the smoke.

Zac watched in amazement as the smoke spiraled on top of their heads in a single, quick motion, then it wafted back into the house, with the visitors in tow.

Zac immediately noticed the distinct coldness and darkness that engulfed them as soon as they entered the room. The door behind them shut all on its own.

"Don't be scared. Follow me," Zac's father's voice came through the darkness.

"I can't even see," Zac whispered back.

He could hear silent whispers and the chilling hissing sounds of unknown sources. The house seemed to be very much alive even though Zac could barely see a thing.

He could hear his father's footsteps in front of him, and so he followed timidly, conscious that he might stumble into a piece of furniture.

"What's this place, Dad?" Zac whispered thinly.

As soon as he said that, a bright light above them suddenly flashed on, and almost twenty other flashlights in different locations turned on, flooding illumination into the room like gushing water.

Zac had to shield his eyes from the sudden light, and it was so frightening that he got knocked off his feet. He heard his father laughing in front of him.

At World's End

"What is this, Dad?" Zac asked, getting to his feet but still shielding his eyes from the bright light.

"This is my friend Dolores' home," Zac's father replied.

Now that Zac's eyes acclimatized to the sudden bright lights, he was able to see just exactly where they were, to his amazement.

They were standing in the middle of a jungle—a jungle that did not seem to have any limits. They were standing on top of green grass—grass that was immaculate and well-manicured, and it stretched into a horizon where Zac could not ascertain the limits.

There were trees and shrubs everywhere, and Zac noticed a small flock of sparrow-like birds flying from tree to tree. The hissing sound was that of crickets and other concealed animals that Zac could not see, and there was a whiff of mint in the air.

Zac was completely unable to understand the sense of space in the place because he was still under the assumption that he was inside a house. After all, he had just walked through a front door.

Zac was completely lost for words as he turned around on the spot and looked around him. His father remained silent for a while, observing his son's reactions and snickering to himself. He was enjoying the sense of befuddlement that had suddenly overcome his son.

At World's End

"What the hell is this place?" Zac asked, for the first time lowering his hood all the way and noticing that there was no door behind them, just more jungle.

His father snickered again.

"I thought we were going to your friend's house", said Zac, trying to take in the strangeness of the place.

"This is her house, alright," replied Zac's father.

"We've never been taught this kind of magic in school, Dad," said Zac. "How is this even possible?"

"Dolores is a practitioner of the highest order of magic in the kingdom, son," said Zac's father. "Only the highest-level wizards in the kingdom can achieve this."

At World's End

Zac was struggling to contain his amazement, watching in the distance as a group of antelopes appeared, walking side-by-side amongst one other and grazing on the beautiful grass.

"This is amazing, Dad."

Zac's father smiled.

"So where is your friend?" Zac asked.

"She'll be along soon enough."

Zac scratched his head. "Where is Mom?"

Zac's father shrugged. "Beats me."

Zac was trying to think about any potential connection between his father and the friend he was about to see. *Was this the reason Mom was not living with them?*

"How is your friend going to help?" Zac asked, suddenly wondering exactly how he would get out of the kingdom.

The smile on Zac's father's face seemed to widen. "Be patient, my son—you'll see."

Zac had a multitude of questions to ask, and just as he was about to shoot another at his dad, a large, trembling sound made him reconsider. Suddenly, the antelopes that were grazing peacefully and unperturbed in the distance started to run away.

They soon disappeared out of sight.

At World's End

The trembling sound grew louder, and Zac could feel a distinct movement approaching them. The sparrow-like birds in the trees flew away, gradually disappearing from sight, too.

"What's that, Dad?" Zac asked. He was feeling panicky.

Zac's father did not answer. The smile had disappeared from his face, and a frown replaced it. He stood there, rooted to the spot, looking up into a very clear and blue sky.

Zac followed his gaze, and just as he was looking up above, he felt a slimy, gripping rope grasp at his leg.

But it was no rope.

At World's End

It was the largest snake Zac had ever seen, weaving its large body in a spiraling fashion around Zac's legs like the smoke that had opened the door for them earlier.

Chapter 3

Zac screamed.

So loud, in fact, it felt as though his lungs would shatter inside of him. The snake was a large green creature, with grey scales teaming its body and its large forked tongue lashing in and out between gigantic fangs.

The snake had very yellow eyes, and its pupils had contracted into slits in the brightness of the surroundings.

"Get it off me!" Zac screamed as the snake weaved itself right to his abdomen, and despite the fact he was clad in just jeans and a heavy jacket, he could feel the wetness of the creature on his body.

At World's End

The snake curled itself comprehensively around Zac, just stopping short of crushing the life out of him. Zac could almost no longer feel his ordinary bodily senses—and instead feeling the drumming of his heart dictate his nervousness.

Then, the snake proceeded to do the oddest thing.

It raised its head, high enough so its slit-eyes were in direct contact with the petrified Zac's dark eyes. Then, in a soft but shrill voice, the snake asked its victim,

"How are you?"

For the first time since the snake attack, Zac managed to throw a glance at his father, noticing for the first time that the older man was watching in silent bemusement, struggling to contain a burst of laughter that seemed ready to come out any time.

"What the hell?" Zac screamed, still in the clutches of the snake.

"Don't be rude," said the snake. "You should respond when you are greeted."

"Get off me!" Zac was becoming hysterical.

The snake seemed to sigh to itself—then, it started uncoiling itself from around Zac. The frightened boy stood there and watched as the snake transformed into a beautiful middle-aged woman in a haze of smoke and hissing sounds.

"Dolores," said Zac's father, stepping forward to meet his host's outstretched hand. "I thought we agreed that you'd stop greeting your guests like that."

Zac was still standing in the same spot, his eyes wide and his mouth agape but without words. He was sweating profusely despite the coolness of the jungle, and he could not seem to set his mind straight on what he had just seen.

"A handsome young boy you have here, Jack," said Dolores, eyeing Zac with a mischievous eye. "He has your eyes, you know."

"W-w-what are you?" stammered Zac. He could still feel the slimy scales of the snake convoluting up his leg.

At World's End

His father laughed out loudly. "This is my son—Zac."

Dolores now stepped forward, standing right in front of Zac and observing him from head to toe. She had a minty smell about her, yellow eyes just like the snake, and she wore a flowing drape-dress that was green in color.

"Your father keeps telling me about you, youknow?" she said in that familiar shrill voice, and Zac was still motionless as she cast her eyes all around him.

"Your father is cruel," she said. "He should have told you what you were walking into."

Zac's father was laughing.

At World's End

Dolores now seized a handful of Zac's hair in her hand, yanking it and causing him some distress.

"Ow," shrieked Zac, "that was painful."

Dolores had a big smile on her lipstick-stained buck teeth. "My apologies, boy."

She let go of Zac, turned around, and started walking towards a big tree nearby.

"Follow me, boys," she said.

Zac remained too rooted to his spot, and only a shove from his father could prompt him to walk towards the tree.

There was a small opening on the base of a tree, no smaller than a mouse-hole. However, Dolores seemed to locate a miniature door which opened and seemed to suck her into the small abyss.

Zac turned to look at his father, petrified.

"Follow her," Zac's father said, that familiar big smile still plastered on his face.

Zac turned to face the tree, and with his eyes closed, he walked forward until he felt a distinct change in the surrounding temperature. Upon opening his eyes, he was surprised to find himself in a small, cramped kitchen, no different from their own back at home.

There was a large fireplace at the end of the room, and it was responsible for half the smoke that rent the air. The other half of the smoke came from a large cigarette set on an ashtray on a dining table in the middle of the room. The cigarette was larger than any that Zac had seen his father smoking, and it seemed to burn with a much thicker smoke.

"Welcome to my humble home," said Dolores, ushering her visitors to worn wooden seats on the far end of the wall that seemed to rely on the wall as part of their structure.

Zac sat down slowly and nervously, watching his father the entire time, uncertain whether he was truly safe.

"Zac," said his father once he had taken a wobbly seat, "Dolores here is going to help you to travel out of the kingdom."

At World's End

Zac's skeptical stance was unchanged. However, he said nothing.

"I'm going to help you get out of here for the time being, and I am the one who will return for you," said Dolores, walking over to the fireplace where a large black pot was brewing a stew.

"Your safety is paramount, son," said Zac's father.

"We're going to fly out of the kingdom at night where no one can see us," said Dolores.

"H-how?" asked Zac, speaking for the first time since meeting her, softly and inaudibly.

"Come again," said Dolores, pausing from stirring her stew for a moment.

At World's End

"You say we'll fly. How?"

Dolores had a large, toothy grin on her craggy face.

"I'll give you wings like a bird."

Chapter 4

The mood in the room was despondent. Zac was more confused than ever, wondering what cryptic message his father's friend was trying to communicate to him.

"I don't understand," he said, for the first time feeling confident enough to address their host directly.

"Like I told you," Zac's father chimed in, "Dolores is one of the highest order witches in the kingdom. You are safest in her hands."

Dolores turned her back on her hosts and continued stirring her stew in her pot. She spent the next five minutes focused on accomplishing this. She then grabbed a serving spoon by the kitchen sink, along with a wooden bowl, and proceeded to serve the stew that she was brewing. She was only serving one wooden plate.

Zac and his father watched in silence as she went along with her responsibility, humming silently to herself and seemingly oblivious for a moment that she had company in the room.

"Well," she said, finally breaking the silence and walking over to Zac, "dinner is served."

She placed the steaming wooden plate before Zac, and it carried a black-grayish liquid substance that looked like porridge. Bubbles were frothing from the stew, even in the wooden plate, and it had the distinct smell of watered-down mint.

At World's End

"What is this?" Zac asked, staring down at his alleged meal. "Why am I eating it alone?"

"I've prepared it, especially for you," said Dolores. "And, oh, before I forget—"

She fished for something on the side-pocket of her dress, revealing some strands of hair.

"I plucked these off your head earlier."

She then stepped forward and placed the hairs into the wooden plate. Zac was watching in amazement.

Suddenly, the plate started shimmering, and the porridge-like substance started to rise up and down the plate, the color changing rapidly, until it was deep red.

At World's End

"What the hell is that?" Zac asked.

The plate stopped bobbing about, and a light steam started to rise from the plate.

"This is your dinner; it will help us get out of the kingdom," Dolores said.

Zac looked down at the goo, mortified by its appearance, and then looked at his father. He was nodding encouragingly, and so Zac gulped down his dinner in record time, seemingly holding his breath in the process.

When Zac was done, he set his spoon down, panting as though he had run a marathon. His father and Dolores were watching him closely, as though waiting for a specific reaction.

At World's End

"I'm sorry Ma'am," said Zac, finally, "but that was not particularly delicious."

Dolores let out a burst of shrill laughter. "Your security concerns me more than your satisfaction, little man."

■■

The Kingdom of Atlantis was in a wreck, harboring all types of crimes and disorders one could conjure.

The capital city, Poseidon, lay in ruins.

The King had ordered all able-bodied men to fight for the survival of the kingdom, and this order had to be implemented by force. Most people were evicted from their homes, their properties stolen, and the cities were destroyed. The excuse that was given by the King to justify this action was that in the event the kingdom is overrun, the enemy will take over an area that has already been destroyed.

Several people were fleeing the island by boat, but the King had eventually passed orders for this to stop. He needed as many subjects as possible on the island to offer support to the defense forces, both technically and morale-wise.

The King was carrying out sacrificial practices and ensured that they remained clandestine, but the rumors that were circulating around the kingdom were most disturbing.

In raids carried out by the king's forces to abduct able-bodied men in the kingdom, teenage boys and younger boys were also being taken in. However, they were systematically disappearing because the defense forces of the kingdom mainly consisted of grown-up men.

The rumors that the King was sacrificing the kingdom's young boys were, at first, disregarded—however, the steady disappearance of a large number of boys, with several families reporting missing children, was a sign of concern for everybody.

Several families were in a panic, and they were using all means available to them to help their children escape a similar fate as the other boys before them.

Zac's father did not elaborate much of this to his son, mainly because he did not want to frighten him. However, he did not give his son much information about his destination or what he was to expect once he had left the kingdom.

Inside the courtyard of the king's residence, there was a large pit constructed that remained ablaze with fire unceasingly. This was the sacrificial pit, and captured boys would be thrown into the pit as prayers and chants to the gods for victory and mercy were incarnated.

The kingdom had been threatened by distant invaders from another kingdom who had initially sent emissaries to the king—all of whom met their deaths.

A war was consequently declared, one that was needless and unnecessary to a majority of the people in the kingdom because they did not even know their enemy. However, the King had done an excellent job of drumming up support for the defense of the kingdom from a "heathen" population that knew nothing but destruction.

The king's own scouts had informed him that a large armada of ships was heading for the kingdom from the large continent to the east—an armada that was exclusively crewed by black people—a race of people who were completely unfamiliar to the peoples of the kingdom.

The King took advantage of this uncertainty and unfamiliarity between his people and the enemy to instigate them into conflict. The future of the kingdom now remained in the balance.

In the house, Zac had started to feel dizzy. His father carried him from the kitchen to a small guest room where there was only a single bed.

"This is the last time I'll see you, for now," he said to Zac once he had set him on the bed. "You'll travel with Dolores, and I'll be seeing you when this war has been won."

Zac felt too tired to reply. The concoction that he had taken was having some effect on his body.

A strange effect.

He felt that his father was leaving him too soon, but he could not seem to muster enough energy to inform his father. A deep headache had developed, and he was feeling tingly all over his body. As his father was

At World's End

speaking to him, he could barely hear him, and his vision was getting affected, too, seeing his father appear in twos and developing a blurry sight.

Zac had no idea that when he awoke, he would be in for the biggest surprise of his life.

Chapter 5

The distinct sound of crows overhead jarred Zac from a deep sleep. He struggled to open his eyes; they seemed welded shut at first, and he felt a strong breeze blowing him back to consciousness.

The first thing he saw when his eyes finally gave way to his will to see was the azure blueness of the sky and the puffy whiteness of the clouds. A strong breeze was blowing directly into his face, and he opened his eyes to realize that he was literally in the sky.

He was lying on top of a large blackbird which was fluffing its feathers and crowing like the nearby crows. The world around them was a clear, blue sky dotted with clouds, and the sun was blazing in the direction they were coming from.

The bird's large feathers made a loud, fluffing sound.

"Hey," Zac started to say, but realize that his own voice was muffled and constrained. He was unable to speak.

His hands reached for his mouth, and he was shocked that he had a beak instead of a mouth. Now that he observed himself a little more closely, his entire body was covered in feathers!

"Hey!" He tried to shout, but no words came out. Instead, his voice seemed muffled and restrained, almost as though he was supposed to crow instead of speak.

At World's End

He tried getting on his feet on top of the large bird that seemed oblivious that he was awake, but he quickly sunk back to his knees, unable to trust his balance.

They were moving fast through the air, and from what he could tell, they had been flying for a long time. He threw a glance at the crows flying alongside the big bird, noticing for the first time that they were flying very high up in the sky, an unusual altitude for crows—and birds, for that matter.

Just as he was about to attempt to shout again and try to understand the conundrum he was in, he noticed that the large bird had a large wound up the side of its leg. It was a gashed wound, a large one—one that could only have been caused by a large, sharp weapon.

"Hey! Bird!" He tried to shout, but it was in vain.

The other crows were cawing loudly now that he was awake, and they seemed to be chattering and jabbering at each other despite the fact that they were in mid-air. He counted four crows in total.

Zac was unsure whether this was his father's way of getting him out of the kingdom. There was a law in the kingdom against teaching and using children for magical purposes. Yet his father had violated an express law for reasons that he still could not understand.

At World's End

The fact that he had feathers and a beak on himself was an indication that some sort of magic spell had been used on him.

Or was it the porridge-like substance that Father's friend fed me? Zac wondered as they soared through the air.

After a while, it started to get cold. Really cold.

And it was not just the strong, passing wind. The temperatures had dropped almost suddenly, and the crows excitable and louder chatters seemed to confirm this.

The big bird let out one large audible crow, shimmied its feathers and seemed to adjust its body position, then changed its flying direction. Its large, yellow beak pointed downwards, and Zac suddenly felt his body being lurched forward and free from the bird.

"Argh!" Zac tried to shout out from the sudden change in direction, but he did not have a mouth.

The bird started to descend rapidly down, the other crows following suit.

Zac tried to shout out once more, but it was an otiose attempt. His grip on the large bird was completely loosened. He could not hang onto the smooth and slippery feathers on the large bird.

Almost inevitably, he felt his body lurch forward, and he was completely thrown off the large bird. The wind was gusting by by him so fast that he could barely make out any other sounds around him.

At World's End

As he plummeted head-first towards the Earth, he noticed the way the sky changed from the fluffy white clouds and eventually into a clear space. The faster he fell and the quicker the wind prattled past him, the colder it seemed to get.

Zac had lost total control of himself, and he knew that only the hard ground would break his fall. He wanted to scream—to shout, but it was impossible.

As they approached the earth, elements of civilization started to appear—cultivated and parted lands, landmarks, and large columns of smoke. The earth was coming faster and faster towards his face, and he braced himself by closing his eyes.

At World's End

In the midst of the descent, the large bird dropped faster than Zac, getting below him in mid-air in order for him to cushion his fall right on its big back.

The landing turned out to be better than Zac would have expected. The large bird landed on its feet, thundering on its great, scaly limbs with Zac struggling to cling onto its back.

They had landed on a sandy beach, with the ocean waters breaking into large waves nearby.

The bird let out a large crow, with the other birds landing on the ground shortly after. They surrounded Zac, who had now dropped off to the dirt.

The birds encircled Zac, screeching as though they were performing some type of ritual. Then, they made

73

a final, loud, screeching noise and took up their wings and flew away.

Zac's heart was still beating quickly, and the sudden fall from the sky had made him nauseous. His head was spinning, and he was in a bit of a panic as he had no idea where he was.

However, he gathered himself, rising to his feet and casting a glance to the sky. The birds had already disappeared into the clouds, out of sight. He also noticed that the feathers on his skin started to fall and fade off by themselves, and he could feel himself regaining control of his mouth.

It was important that he understood where he was. His father had not given him much information, and

At World's End

he had no idea which part of the world he had flown

to.

He turned around to start walking inland.

But his way was blocked by a towering, sky-high ice

boulder.

Chapter 6

Zac started up in the sky, surprised and confused at the same time. A heavenly body similar to the sun was shining somewhere up in the clouds, and he was standing on a beach. Yet there was a large ice boulder right in his way.

When he examined more closely, he realized that the ice boulder stretched all the way to the horizon on both sides. There was no immediate and apparent way of getting around it.

Am I going to have to climb this? Zac thought to himself, looking behind him at the sight of the clear, blue sea. He could see no way forward or backward. He was trapped between a sea and a large ice boulder.

At World's End

The feathers that were on his skin, and the beak that was his mouth, had now fully disappeared. He was a normal human being once more, but that did not console him much.

He decided that the only way he was going to stay alive was by climbing the ice boulder and getting to the other side. He still could not understand why his father would sanction such an ungainly departure from home to a location of which he had no idea.

The ice boulder was freezing cold when Zac put his hand on it. He looked up to its heights, wondering how he was going to climb it. It was a smooth column of white ice, rising almost to the clouds, like the fence around a giant's house.

At World's End

Just as he was contemplating the best course of action for himself to take, the ice right in front of him started melting rapidly.

So rapidly that it seemed to be boring a hole through the boulder. As Zac stood there watching in incredulity, the ice in front of him melted away and formed a cave-like dome, a doorway through it.

Without hesitating, and leaving the crashing waves behind him, Zac walked into the hole, his heart beating very fast. He was unsure what was going on, but he had already seen enough to be certain that the world he once knew was no more.

The inside of the boulder was extremely cold, and there was a hissing noise as the hole melted away the ice right to the other side. Zac crept through it quickly and emerged on the other side, right into the embrace of a short old man.

"Huh?" Zac gasped in surprise, losing his footing and landing comfortably on the arms of the old man.

"Zac, my boy," he said in a loud booming voice, propping Zac back on his feet with his surprisingly strong arms. He was holding a wooden cane in his right hand. "I'm glad you've arrived safely."

Zac was unsure what was going on. Once he gained his composure, he studied the man standing in front of him, as well as the surprising landscape behind him.

At World's End

"Who are you?" Zac asked. The old man had a long, white beard and blue, intrusive eyes that were buried in a scraggly face. He wore a large, white overhanging coat.

They were standing on the snowy ground, several inches thick because of continuous snowfall. The entire landscape before Zac was an utter surprise because it was a continuous ice sheet spreading into the horizon. A strong wind seemed to be constantly blowing, and it gave the entire place the appearance of a landscape hit by a blizzard. Apart from the old man standing before him, Zac could not see any other color before them but white.

"Where am I?" Zac asked.

At World's End

The old man stared back at Zac with a frown. "Your father wouldn't even tell you. Did he?"

Zac frowned as well. "Tell me what?"

The old man seemed to shut his eyes, as if in disappointment, then instructed Zac, "Follow me."

He turned around and started walking in the other direction. Zac was unsure of what to do—what had just happened. He stared behind him, noticing that the hole that had developed in the ice boulder had now disappeared and was replaced by a sheet of ice.

The old man was walking away slowly and steadily, and Zac realized that he had no choice. He raced up to the old man to join him.

"Who are you?" Zac asked. "At the very least, you can tell me that."

The old man turned his deep blue eyes in Zac's direction, and the young boy felt the eyes bore into his body.

"You're my grandpa, aren't you?" Zac asked.

The old man smiled, taking his eyes off Zac. "Call me 'Grandpa.'"

Zac felt slightly relieved. "Dad said that I was coming to visit you. I'm glad I've found you. How did you find me, anyway?"

At World's End

The old man was trudging along slowly. His coat was sweeping behind him, like a wedding dress, and it made an invisible trail on the white snowy ground.

"Your father told me that you'd be along," said Grandpa.

"How?" Zac asked. "He didn't come with me."

Grandpa smiled. "There is a special way for us to communicate despite the distance."

"Where am I, anyway, Grandpa?" asked Zac, stumbling on some ice and almost losing his footing.

"Be careful," said Grandpa. "It has been snowing for six days straight, and as you can see, there has been a very heavy snowfall."

At World's End

Zac nodded in agreement.

"This is the South Pole," said Grandpa, "our home."

Zac frowned. "I thought that our family originally came from Atlantis."

Grandpa frowned. "Is that what your father has told you? Shameful of him to say."

Grandpa seemed to shake his head to himself, silently muttering to himself as Zac felt more confused than ever. He sensed that there was some kind of problem between his father and his grandfather, but he could not tell what it was.

"Dad told me that you and Grandma used to live in Atlantis," said Zac. "Then you left."

At World's End

"That's true," said Grandpa, as Zac noticed a small countryhouse appearing out of the whiteness in the distance. Grandpa continued, "Atlantis was once where your grandmother and I lived, but it was never home to begin with."

"Where's that?" Zac asked, pointing.

"Home," was the solitary response from Grandpa.

Zac was slightly surprised. He was looking around, but apart from the small house, he could not see any other signs of life or indication that somebody else other than Grandpa might be living here. "Do you live here alone with Grandma?"

Grandpa stopped short of his tracks, grabbing Zac by the shoulder and bringing him, too, to a sudden halt.

At World's End

The wind was blowing almost quicker now, and more snow was getting into Zac's eyes.

"Huh?" Exclaimed Zac.

"Listen to me carefully, "said Grandpa, his eyes had widened, and he had a very exasperated look on his face. "This happens to be a very dangerous place, and you'll be doing yourself a very big favor to not leave that house again once you get in it."

Chapter 7

The inside of the small cabin house turned out to be another big surprise for Zac. He could not seem to go long before he stumbled onto something that he had never in his life seen before.

From the outside, the small cabin house was a small space—a bungalow occupying not more than a few square feet; however, the inside of the house resembled a castle, complete with a miniature moat that led to the living sections of the house.

The sheer size of the house completely surprised Zac. From the foyer, as Grandpa closed the front door, he could already tell that the entire complex must have at least one hundred rooms. There were at least five floors in the house.

"How is this possible?" Zac asked.

And there was more.

The house was much warmer than the outside, and there were loud, thundering sounds coming from somewhere above—in the upper floors of the house.

"What is that?" Zac asked.

Grandpa removed his large white coat and hanged it by the door. It was dripping wet.

"Do you live in this house alone with Grandma?" Zac's questions were endless.

At World's End

Grandpa did not answer. Instead, he gingerly walked into a dark room that turned out to be the living room, leaving paddled footsteps in his trail on the garnished floor.

Zac followed, walking through the dark room, and he could make out the silhouette of horned animal heads on the walls, furniture, and heavily draped windows.

The door at the far end led to a surprisingly well-lit kitchen that was sparkling white with a beautiful wooden dinner table in the middle of the room. There was a large black pot steaming at the far end of the room, surprisingly similar to that he had seen in the home of Dolores.

At World's End

However, the main thing that caught Zac's eye was a graceful old woman tending to her cooking on the kitchen counter close to a picturesque window. She was slicing through a number of vegetables on a chopping board, and when Grandpa and Zac walked in, she dropped all she was doing, hastily wiped her hands on her apron and signaled for Zac to come to her.

"Come here, son," she said in a croaky but satisfied voice, "We have been waiting for you."

She walked over to Zac and clutched him in a strong embrace, surprising the young boy with the strength that she had.

At World's End

"I realize that you don't know us," Grandma said, nodding in Grandpa's direction. Grandpa had taken a seat at the dinner table and was just starting to pore over a newspaper. "But we were there when you were born. We watched you grow up until we left."

"Sit down, son," she said, "I'll whip up something for you to eat. The journey here must have made you hungry."

Zac took a seat next to his grandfather, who was engrossed his newspaper.

"Are there other people here?" Zac asked.

"Yes, this is a large village," said Grandma.

At World's End

Grandpa looked up from his newspaper momentarily. "Probably the biggest village in the world."

"Does it always snow in the South Pole?" Zac asked quizzically. Grandma was rapidly whisking something in a bowl that was out of sight for Zac, but he felt confident that he would not be presented with a questionable porridge-like substance.

"Yes, it does, son," said Grandma. "Non-stop."

Aren't you going to ask me what is happening back at home?" Zac asked.

Grandpa lifted his eyes from his newspaper once more to stare down at Zac. Grandma momentarily paused what she was doing, then went on as though she had not broken a sweat.

At World's End

"We know," Grandpa said. He went back to burying his face in between the pages of the internationals.

"How do you get newspapers here?" Zac asked, starting to realize that they were practically in the middle of nowhere.

"We've already told you, son," said Grandma. "This is a big village. There's everything here."

"I don't get it, Grandma," said Zac. "When we were coming here with Grandpa, I didn't see a thing. I mean, the whole place is just—"

Zac was cut off by a large booming noise coming from the upper sections of the house. It was so loud it seemed to be accompanied by a large crash, like the noise of multiple windows breaking.

At World's End

Grandpa raised his head, looking at the ceiling. Grandma was busying herself with preparing the meal. She was crisscrossing the room without commenting.

The large, booming noise happened again, this time louder, and created a slight tremor in the house.

"What was that?" Zac asked. It seemed appropriate that he be the one to speak.

"Can I have something to eat?" Grandpa asked, turning in the direction of Grandma and ignoring Zac's question.

"You have nothing to worry about, son," said Grandma, walking over to the table and setting a plate down before Zac. It was a sumptuous beef stew with potatoes and some greens. Grandma also set a similar plate for Grandpa before him.

"Eat!" Grandma declared, observing closely as Zac reached for his spoon and took a dig at the food.

"This is actually quite good, Grandma," said Zac, shoveling mouthfuls of the relieving food into his mouth.

The loud, crashing sounds happened twice while they were eating, and Grandpa made sure to eat hastily before leaving in a rush.

"Be careful," Grandma shouted at him as he left the room, making Zac even more nervous.

"What is it, Grandma?" Zac asked.

Grandma smiled, joining him on the dining table after placing Grandpa's dishes in the sink. She sat down heavily.

"You have nothing to worry about, son," said Grandma, "Grandpa will take care of it."

There was another large, crashing noise. Then, a screeching scream.

Grandpa's scream.

Zac stumbled to his feet now, his heart racing and his eyes wide in bewilderment.

"That's Grandpa," he said. "Should we go and help?"

At World's End

Grandma was about to respond, but just as she was,

the lights suddenly went out and the entire house was

doused in pitch blackness.

Chapter 8

Outside the small country-house, a blizzard was raging over the frozen landscape and the darkness of the night attempted to blacken the whiteness of the surrounding.

Inside the house, it was pitch black, and everything had suddenly gone silent.

Zac was still on his feet, frightened by the sudden disappearance of the lights. Grandma appeared motionless. Even she seemed surprised by the abrupt turn of events.

"That's odd," her scraggly voice floated to Zac through the darkness. "That has never happened before."

At World's End

"W-what about Grandpa?" Zac asked. He was frightened, and he felt himself trembling. "Is he going to be alright?"

"Of course, he will," said Grandma, and even Zac could tell that her voice was frightened and that she was afraid of revealing this fact.

She got to her feet and shuffled to the other side of the room. She bumped into several things, such as the chairs and the dinner table, but she ultimately reached her destination and flickered on a wand. It emitted a low glow of light from its tip.

Her face appeared as if completely out of the darkness, and she pointed the wand in Zac's direction as though to confirm that he was still there. The frightened young boy was standing over his seat by the dinner table, trembling.

"Sit down, son," she said, "I'll go check on your grandfather."

Zac was wary about sitting alone in the dark in a kitchen he was not familiar with.

"Can I just come with you?" He asked.

He watched his grandmother's face twist slightly as though looking for the right words to stop him. However, she seemed to resign to what was evidently inevitable.

"Follow me," she said, "but stay close."

At World's End

Zac stumbled after his grandmother, and he could barely make out the house in the darkness as they stepped into the next room. There was a strong hint of mint in the air, and all he could make out were different sets of furniture.

"I'm sorry that your first night has to be filled with lots of drama," whispered Grandma, creeping forward and opening the door to the darkened room.

"It's okay, Grandma," Zac whispered back.

The house was so large—Zac had no idea that a blizzard was raging outside nor that there were very strong winds whizzing through the icy landscape. The entire house was engulfed in a raging snowstorm that tempted to swallow it in its swirling, twisting chasm.

At World's End

The door that Grandma opened led into a narrow, winding stairwell that led to the very top of the house. The stairwell was made of metallic meterial, and when Grandma started wobbling up the first few steps, a loud, banging noise emanated from them.

The miniature illumination coming from Grandma's wand was almost unhelpful for Zac, and he had to stay close to his grandmother in order to go forward.

They did not speak as they noisily climbed up the stairs. The house had become eerily quiet, and the loud crashing noises from before seemed to have altogether disappeared.

As they climbed the stairs, Zac noticed that there were doors at regular intervals up their climb. When they reached the third door, Grandma opened it, and they stepped into a narrow, unlit hallway.

Oddly enough, Grandma secured the door behind them - the door to the stairwell before - proceeding through the darkened room to another door at the far end.

In this room, Zac could not see anything at all, partly because of the poor illumination, and partly because of its sheer, large size. The items in the room were distant from each other and practically impossible to see in the sheer darkness.

"This way," Grandma said in an undertone that reverberated through the blackness.

At World's End

Zac was not sure whether he should be scared or curious. The door out of the room emerged to another long, stretching hallway.

Zac could not see, but from what he could tell in the darkness, they were standing in the longest section of the house. There was a slight breeze blowing through it, and this was probably from a window at one of the extremes of the large hallway.

"W-where is Grandpa?" Zac's frightened voice was barely audible to Grandma. And she chose to ignore it.

She remained silent as she started trudging down the hallway, Zac hesitantly following behind her. Zac could not see a thing, and he felt the intensity of his heartbeat increase with every step he took.

Suddenly, looming in the darkness and standing facing the opposite direction in front of them in the middle of the hallway, a large, towering dark figure was heaving in and out heavily.

Grandma stopped short on her feet, so brusquely that Zac bumped into her.

The large figure in front of them did not move—it remained motionless, heaving in and out. Zac could hear the distinct whooshing of air as it rushed in and out of the figure's lungs.

"I think we need to get out of here," Zac said, his heart racing rapidly. He could not see in the dark that

At World's End

Grandma's face had stiffened into a frown. However, she did not say anything.

The figure turned around in the dark, and Zac could distinctly see a large, shining cleaver in its hands.

"Grandpa?" Zac called out. He could almost tell Grandpa's body shape through the darkness. However, the figure remained unresponsive, the cleaver still clung on its hands.

Then, without warning, the figure started to move forward, so quickly that Zac, who had already resolved to start running back in the direction they came, stumbled and lost his balance.

As he crashed to the dusty floor, he saw the figure rush towards Grandma and clutch her by her chin.

At World's End

"No!" Zac shouted, immediately getting back to his feet.

But the large, shiny cleaver was already being pointed directly in his face.

Chapter 9

"Why have you brought him up here?" The cold voice of the figure jeered at Grandma. The cleaver was pointed at Zac's face—then, the figure slowly dropped its arm.

In the midst of the confusion, Grandma had dropped her wand, and the illuminating tip shone brightly on the dusty concrete floor. She bent over to pick up the wand and raised it to the figure's face, revealing the disgruntled face of Grandpa in the darkness.

"It's dangerous up here," he said, still clutching the cleaver in his hand threateningly.

Grandma then pointed her wand behind Grandpa, trying to illuminate what was behind him. But from

108

where Zac was standing, he could barely see anything else at the other end of the hall.

"Let's get out of here," said Grandpa, walking past Grandma. He turned to Zac. "You should never come up here while you are living in this house. I hope that is clear."

He then shuffled past Zac, walking slowly in the direction that they had come.

Grandma sighed heavily, still pointing the wand in front of her, then she turned and set off after Grandpa.

Zac could not seem to understand what was happening in this weird house in the middle of nowhere.

"Come," Grandma said to him, "I'll show you where you'll be sleeping for the night."

▪▪▪

The next morning, Zac emerged from his large room that was on the first floor, into the kitchen to find both his grandparents at the dinner table in the kitchen.

The kitchen almost looked the same as the previous night, with the main difference being the source of light coming in from a closed kitchen window. The whiteness of the snow outside was sufficient to illuminate the kitchen with adequate light.

Grandpa was seated quietly, reading that morning's newspaper. He only raised his eyes once when Zac strode into the room, then resumed burying his face in the pages.

"Morning, son," said Grandma, a much more cheerful look on her face than the previous night. "Get yourself something to eat."

She pointed to the kitchen counter where there was a steaming kettle and a platter with different kinds of food.

"What will you do while you're here?" Grandma asked as Zac set about serving himself something to eat.

He shrugged his shoulders.

"What's there to do?"

At World's End

"You can help your grandfather do some cleaning in the garage," Grandma said, motioning her head in Grandpa's direction. "You can also help me do cleaning here in the house. I'll be going to the synagogue later on when it's a bit warmer than it is."

Zac looked outside the window to the emptiness of the whiteness outside.

"Does it get warmer?"

Grandma laughed slightly. "I realize it's hard to imagine," she said, "but when you have lived here long enough, it is possible to tell even when there is a slight change in temperature."

Zac took a seat on the dinner table, clutching in his hand a small plate and a steaming cup.

At World's End

"I think I'll just look around," said Zac, "explore the place."

Grandpa looked up from his newspaper once again, briefly, with a big frown on his face.

Grandma smiled widely at Zac.

"You're a curious one, aren't you?" She asked.

Zac was enjoying his breakfast.

"What choice do I have?"

■■

After breakfast, Zac found himself outside in a moderately cold environment, with the shape and proportion of the house he had slept in the previous night completely baffling him.

At World's End

He stood a few meters from the front porch of the house. There was no fencing around the house, and neither did it look sophisticated, but the inside of the house was a totally different experience. He had been raised in a magical world, but the very magical details that he encountered in his grandparents' home was nothing short of astounding.

There was the howling sound of a passing breeze, but the sound was always constant and unyielding. Zac simply could not understand how there could be life in this place, with the cold so discouraging and the emptiness so desolate.

His grandma had told him that there were other homes and a synagogue towards the right side of the house. She had told him that he would be able to find other people along the track—other youngsters, in fact, that he might socialize with.

This prospect made him happy because he could not understand how he was going to bear a holiday all by himself in this ice desert. This was compounded by the fact that he had no idea what was going on back at home, whether he would ever be able to return and see his father and mother once again.

Zac started to amble in the general direction east of the house. He was looking forward to meeting up with his age mates and finding out what he could do in this place.

As he walked, all he could see was whiteness. After about twenty minutes, he was both surprised and saddened by the fact that he could not see his grandparents' house, but neither had he come across any satisfactory signs of life.

But just as he was starting to lose hope and resolve to go back to the house, he started hearing another distinct sound above the howling noise of the wind.

A much scarier sound.

It was the sound of hooves crunching over the open, snowy landscape—the sound of multiple hooves approaching in his direction.

Zac's eyes widened, looking around him, but he could not see anything. All he could see was the whiteness of the surrounding. Instinctively, he started running in

the opposite direction of the sounds of the
approaching hooves.

He started feeling like he did the previous day all over
again—the nervousness, the heart racing, the disbelief
and contempt for what he could not see was posing
danger to him.

The sounds of the approaching hooves were getting
louder as he started to run across the snow. He
needed help, but he could not see anything in the
whiteness.

Every time he threw his eyes behind his shoulder, he
could not see any animals chasing him. However, the
distinct sound of their approaching menace was
audible enough for Zac.

Then, up ahead, as though springing out of the darkness, a small shed-like structure appeared before him. It was made of clustered wooden walls and a corrugated metal roof.

Zac felt a slight tinge of hope cast itself within him, and he quickened his pace, hoping he could get to the shed before whatever danger besetting him got to him.

But the shed was so far away, and Zac could only run so fast. It was inevitable that he would lose his balance when he was just a few meters away from the shed, critically, just when the sounds of the hooves had got close enough.

At World's End

"Nooo!" Zac shouted as he plunged face-first into the thick snow.

The invisible animals that were giving chase closed in on Zac.

Chapter 10

Once on the ground, Zac was almost immediately able to confirm his worst fears. The approaching animals had already surrounded him and were snarling and growling, just like a pack of dogs, and they were very intimidating in the aggressive steps they were taking towards him.

However, as Zac braced himself from an attack by raising his hands to his face, he noticed the oddest thing—he could not see the animals.

He could almost feel the hot, malodorous breath of the animals as they circled around him—growling ominously and making loud, crunching sounds as they were traversing the snow.

At World's End

But they were invisible - completely out of sight - and Zac felt that this was the most threatening aspect of their peril. He could not tell what type of animal they were. The sounds of their menacing growls made him assume that there were at least half a dozen of them.

"What kind of magic is this?" Zac muttered to himself under his breath, lowering his hands, realizing that he had no chance to defend himself. He was out in the open, surrounded by an invisible enemy, and all he could do was watch in horror.

As the invisible threat prepared to manifest itself, Zac heard approaching footsteps from behind him. Looking over his shoulder, he saw a short girl racing towards him, her hand outstretched, clutching a wand. She was flickering it in Zac's direction, and he immediately noticed the growling noises disappearing one-by-one.

By the time the girl got to him, the growling noises had almost completely disappeared. She stretched out the other hand.

"Come with me," she said. "We're not out of the woods yet."

Zac was a little surprised.

He looked at the stranger before him—a girl no older or younger than him, dressed in a slick dress and a light, white top. She had eyes bluer than the sky, and a beautiful, shapely physique.

At World's End

Realizing that he had no choice, considering the imminent threat bearing down upon him, Zac grabbed her outstretched hand, and she pulled him up from the ground. He had to brush snow off from his bottom.

"Let's take shelter in that old farmhouse," she said, pointing to the shed that Zac had earlier spotted. "Quickly!"

They raced across the ice, Zac tumbling in the deeper sections of the snow. They got to the door in a wave of relief, the girl getting there first, yanking the old door to the shed open, almost off its hinges and stumbling into the security of the darkness inside.

At World's End

Zac closed the door behind them, pushing it shut with his back against it. The girl flicked her wand in the darkness, and just like Zac had seen with Grandma's wand, a small glow was emitted from its tip and it provided faint illumination.

Zac sunk to his knees—panting and trying to brush off the snow on his clothes. His heart was racing profusely, and despite the coldness of the place, he had beads of sweat clinging on his face like pierced earrings.

The girl had a dubious and frowned look on her face, and she stared down at Zac for a moment before he realized this.

At World's End

"Who are you?" The girl asked, trying as much as possible to be polite to the stranger.

Zac looked up at her, studying the wand which she was now pointing directly at him. It was a thin black stick, no longer than a thirty-centimeter ruler but seemed significantly less thick than that he had seen with Grandma.

He got up to his feet, warily putting his eyes on the girl. He realized that he could barely see anything else in the shed, and the only sounds he could hear were the whooshing sounds of the wind outside.

"I'm Zac," he said, "I'm here for a visit."

The girl still had the sternest frown on her face.

At World's End

"I came to this place just yesterday," said Zac.

"This is not a place for visiting," she said in a gruff voice. "Nobody is allowed to come here."

Zac raised his eyelids in surprise, wondering what to say.

"Who are you?" He finally asked after a long pause.

The girl remained standing there quietly and pointed her wand directly at Zac. She seemed unsure of what to say, as though she was looking for the right words to address Zac.

"I've been trying to find somebody to tell me what the hell is going on here," Zac said, staring at the girl's eyes. "My grandparents won't tell me a thing."

At World's End

The girl's eyes seemed to light up.

"Those are your grandparents living down this road, the small farmhouse with the red roof?" She asked.

Zac nodded with a smile. "Yes. That's them."

The girl smiled as well. "I didn't realize." She stopped pointing her wand at Zac and instead, gave him her right hand.

"I'm Valeria."

"Zac; it's a pleasure to meet you, and thanks for saving me."

Both stared at each other for a moment as if acknowledging each other's presence.

"This is a dangerous place," said Valeria. "Why did your grandparents allow you to come outside alone?"

Zac shrugged. "There's nothing to do in their house."

Valeria laughed, so loudly that for a second Zac thought the noise would invite the animals chasing at him to return.

"What were those animals that were chasing me earlier?" Zac asked.

"Those are barking ghosts," Valeria said, a serious look developing on her face. "They are an extremely dangerous pack of invisible dogs. You are lucky I was here—they would have ripped you apart without you even seeing them."

At World's End

Zac's eyes widened.

Valeria got closer to him. "That's not the most serious problem in this place, though."

Zac remained motionless and silent.

"I don't know why you have come here now at this moment," said Valeria, "but I don't see how you'll get out of here alive."

Chapter 11

"What do you mean?" Zac asked. He was trying to make something of the serious expression that was developing on Valeria's face, and her words were utterly cold and chilly, just like the snow dripping off Zac's wet clothes.

Valeria shook her head. "Nobody has told you where this is, right?"

Zac shrugged and nodded at the same time.

"Well," said Valeria, "I'll show you."

There was a loud sound of the gust of wind outside rising high up in the air and carrying with it slivers of snow. There was a sudden, terrific great wind that pounded snow on the wooden door and walls of the shed.

"We shouldn't stay long in here," said Valeria, "I was actually walking towards the Western Wall. Would you like to come?"

"Why not?" Responded Zac.

Valeria reached for the door, reaching close enough to Zac for him to feel the hint of lavender on Valeria's white top. She opened the door slowly and meticulously, sticking her head outside to survey the snowy outside as the strong winds subsided.

"What did you do to those 'dogs'?" Zac asked. He raised both his index fingers in a vertical motion when he said the word 'dogs.'

131

"I confused them," said Valeria, sticking her head back into the shed. "There is a specific magic spell for that."

She looked at Zac more closely.

"Where do you come from?" She asked. "Don't you use magic?"

Zac shrugged. "Where I'm from, people are not allowed to use magic until they are eighteen years of age."

"Oh my God," said Valeria, raising her left hand to her mouth and her eyes bulging out from their sockets. "Don't tell me you're from the infamous kingdom of Atlantis."

At World's End

Zac smiled.

"It's so very sad," said Valeria, "what you're missing, what you can do with magic."

"Can you show me?"

Valeria let out a laugh. "Well," she said, "you're in good hands. And there are no restrictions on the use of magic here. No laws. In fact, I don't think human beings would be able to live here without magic."

Zac could not understand. "Why?"

Valeria smiled. "I'll show you, don't worry. Do you mind telling me why you came here?"

"There's a war back home," Zac said. "My father sent me here until it is over."

Valeria smiled. "That's understandable. Without magic, there's nothing you'd be able to do."

She reached for the door once again. "Follow me. I'll take you to the most interesting place in the South Pole. It might help answer some questions for you."

She pulled open the door, surveyed the area quickly, and jumped outside into the cold. Zac followed suit.

They raced across the snow in the direction that Zac had come earlier. He now felt confident and happy racing through the snow as he was not alone, and he had at least found somebody to talk to.

They ran for almost twenty minutes, Zac struggling to keep up with Valeria who obviously glided through the snow with greater ease. She had been in the South

At World's End

Pole for a long time, and had adapted to living in an icy environment.

Even though there was snow everywhere, it seemed to get colder with every step they took. At some point, Valeria pointed towards her left, indicating loudly to Zac, "I think your grandparents' house is somewhere in that direction."

Zac could not tell because the entire landscape looked all the same to him. They might have been running straight for more than twenty minutes, but all he noticed in the changing landscape was the thickness of the snow covering in different parts of the area.

Zac was starting to feel quite exhausted, and the harder the deep breaths he took, the colder he felt.

The surrounding also seemed to change. The whiteness was slowly being consumed by a strange blackness, and Zac started noticing for the first time that there were large, black boulders concealing themselves in the thickness of the snow cover.

The sound of the whooshing wind was even louder, and there was a sense of hazard tingling somewhere inside Zac.

Are the invisible hounds nearby? He asked himself. *What the hell is it with this place?*

"Where are you taking me?" He shouted to Valeria. She had already gained some ground ahead of him.

She stopped where she was and turned around to Zac, waving at him and indicating to him to hurry up.

At World's End

When he caught up to her, he felt that he could not be able to bear the cold anymore.

"W-why has it gotten so cold?" He asked Valeria.

Valeria had a smile on her face. She did not seem to be so perturbed by the cold as was Zac.

"We're getting closer," she said. The winds seemed to be blowing even stronger here, and Valeria had to speak up so that the stricken Zac could hear her.

"I can't believe how cold it has become," said Zac, his teeth chattering non stop.

Valeria started walking on, but more slowly. The strong winds were inhibiting them from moving quickly.

At World's End

Then Zac noticed it, at first rejecting what he had seen, then settling on the horror of the reality:

Before them, stretching on in endless darkness, there was a large void, like the crater of a volcanic mountain, so large that there were clouds hanging right above ground level.

Zac noticed that Valeria had brought him to the edge of an enormous pit, and he realized why he started to feel much colder. Valeria had already gotten right to the edge of the pit, but Zac was struggling to catch up with her, partly because of the horror of where they were and partly because the winds were blowing so strong now that they were throwing up snow and rocky dust in Zac's face.

At World's End

Zac tried to shout something to Valeria, but his words got sucked up in the strong winds and blew away into the swirling snow. By the time Zac got to Valeria's location, he could barely conceal his shock.

The bare emptiness of the place was astounding. Zac had gotten so used to the whiteness of his surrounding, the sudden appearance of the blackness of the void was difficult to take.

Valeria could see the shock on Zac's face. It amused her. The strong winds blowing were causing strange sounds to emanate from the cold darkness below.

They were close enough to the edge, but Zac did not dare go any closer, noticing that the edges of the pit seemed to extend into the horizon in a circular

manner.

"Welcome to the end of the world," Valeria said in a

soft voice.

Chapter 12

The strong winds were rifling through Zac's black hair, and this seemed to have no effect on his surprise. The daunting darkness before him was very intimidating, and the fact that anything was barely visible made it even more frightening.

Zac looked at Valeria who was staring ahead and seemed to be taking in the strange scenery in a different appreciation. She was breathing heavily in delight, and there was a large smile plastered on her face.

"What do you mean 'the end of the world'?" Zac asked.

"Exactly that," replied Valeria, "can't you see?"

At World's End

Zac looked straight ahead, but all he could see was darkness.

"There's nothing beyond here", Valeria said, indicating to Zac the edge of the pit. "This is where the world we know stops."

"How come I've never heard of this before?" Zac asked, "Is this some sort of magic?"

Valeria laughed.

Zac again struggled to look through the darkness, but to no avail.

"Why would my father send me here?" Zac asked aloud.

At World's End

"This is the safest place you can be," Valeria said, turning to study Zac. "It actually makes perfect sense why your father sent you here. Nobody can get to you here."

Zac stared into the darkness of the void, several questions still racing through his head. Everything he had seen since his father asked him to travel here was out of the ordinary—things he had never before seen in his life.

The coldness of the place was astounding. The howling of the wind below them seemed to be getting louder.

"We'll have to get back," Valeria said. "We're actually not allowed to come out this far—to the edge."

"Tell me something, then," said Zac. "Is there land beyond this point—other life out there?"

Valeria turned to look him squarely in the eye. "That's a secret."

Zac frowned. "What's so secret about that? Why won't you just let me know?"

"I have an ancient book that will answer all your questions," said Valeria. "Let's go back, and I'll show you."

Zac nodded. He looked up at the sky and noticed that it was heavily clouded. Any light coming from the sky was stifled by the clouds like a blanket smothering a young baby to sleep.

At World's End

Valeria turned around and started walking slowly back in the direction they had come. Zac followed suit slowly, looking over at the dark edge one more time.

As they started walking slowly back, this time the wind behind them—a very loud bellowing noise, made Zac stop dead in his tracks and turn around. Even Valeria was alarmed by the sudden bellowing clamor that seemed to be coming from the darkness below the edge, halting in her tracks as well.

Zac's curiosity had already made him take the first step back towards the edge, but he had not noticed that Valeria was suddenly the one on edge. Her eyes had almost swollen out of their sockets, and she was staring ominously into the space ahead of them.

"Zac," she started to say, then reached forward quickly and grabbed him by the shoulder. "Our lives are in danger."

Zac's eyes also bulged when he realized just how serious Valeria was from the expression on her face.

"Run!"

Once again, Zac found himself running for dear life, stumbling along the rocky terrain before getting to the snow-covered sections of the ground. With the wind behind them, Zac felt more confident running faster and in tandem with Valeria.

However, he did not understand what they were running away from—but judging from the frightened look on Valeria's face, he did not want to stick around to find out.

He was starting to understand his grandfather's warning earlier when he had told Zac that the South Pole was not a particularly safe place. This was turning out to be the strangest "holiday" for Zac because he was spending most of it sprinting away from one hazard and into another.

The bellowing sound behind them was accompanied by a compelling whooshing sound, and there was a disturbingly loud, cracking sound behind them that launched a large chunk of snow along with black rocks high into the air.

At World's End

Zac stole a glance behind him, and he was shocked to see that the ground they had been standing on earlier had formed into a depression, with a large crack all the way to the edge having been developed.

As he was looking behind him while running forward, Zac again stumbled in the deepening snow cover of the ground and lost his balance.

"Valeria!" He shouted as he felt his entire body lurch forward, his feet completely setting off the ground. He landed with a heavy thud into the rocky-cum-snow-covered ground.

Valeria had come to a screeching halt and was starting to tumble back towards Zac desperately.

At World's End

While on the ground, Zac noticed that a large, white, steam-like haze was rising from below the edge into the air, so high it that it was dispersing the puffy clouds directly above it.

The bellowing sound seemed to be getting louder, and in the process, a deep bass hum accompanied it. Consequently, tremors emanated on the rocky ground that manifested themselves in large visible cracks that stretched across the rocky terrain.

Valeria grabbed Zac's shoulders and pulled him up.

"Move!" She shouted at him.

Once on his feet, Zac started running again, but this time without looking back. He was already terrified enough of the ground developing rapid cracks that could consume them at any moment.

He followed Valeria as they burst out onto the snowy terrain, the bellowing sounds growing even louder and the tremors posing a bigger threat.

"What the hell is that?" Zac screamed at Valeria, but she was too busy running for her life to focus on giving a reply.

Suddenly, there was a large, banging sound behind them, right on the rocks, and this time when Zac threw a glance behind him to see what they were fleeing from, he started hoping that he never did so.

At World's End

He saw a giant green hand slamming the ground from the edge, oozing black-greenish liquid from its enormous fingers.

Chapter 13

The large, green slimy monster stretched its gigantic hand over the rough terrain, boosting its heaving body up from the depths of the ground and its large, horned head appearing above ground.

The monster had deep yellow eyes the size of basketballs, and his large pupils rolled to stare down at the fleeing youngsters, still supporting its weight over the edge of the land with its hand. It let out another loud bellow that sent shattering shockwaves throughout the place.

"You two," it shouted, much to the surprise and disbelief of Zac, "stop where you are!"

At World's End

But the fleeing youngsters made no inclination to stop, and instead, they scrambled even faster over the snow and disappeared into the distance.

Zac was hysterical, screaming and running at the same time. Almost everything he had assumed he knew was shattering before him, and all he could think of at that point was running even faster.

"Let's head for your grandparent's house," Valeria shouted over the crunching sounds of their shoes in the snow. "It's the closest place to us now."

"What the hell is that thing?" Zac shouted back, but his words seemed to disappear in the gale-force wind.

They kept running until the familiar farmhouse came into view in the distance. Zac did not stop running until he was on the front porch of the house. Upon looking back, all they could see was the snow rising in the air—courtesy of the robust winds. They had left visible, scrambled footprints that stretched into the distant whiteness.

Valeria knocked on the door, anxiously at first, and then she pounded on it. She was just as nervous as Zac.

"That thing could talk," Zac shouted at Valeria even though she was standing right in front of him. "What the hell was that?"

"That's what we're all afraid of," Valeria replied, knocking on the door again.

At World's End

"What kind of animal is that?" Zac could not stop the flow of questions gushing from his mouth like a burst pipe spewing its water haphazardly.

Valeria knocked on the door again, suddenly realizing that there was probably nobody in the house to answer the door.

"Zac," Valeria started to say.

"You have to tell me what the hell is going on here," Zac said, his eyes wide and his voice delirious.

"Zac," Valeria said again, "are your grandparents in?"

Zac stopped with his flurry of questions for a moment, realizing that they had been standing on the porch far longer than he would have wished to.

At World's End

Valeria had been knocking on the door long enough, yet they were still standing outside in the freezing cold.

Were his grandparents not home?

He reached for the door handle and pulled the door open. The eerie darkness of the hallway greeted them, and they quickly ushered themselves inside away from the cold.

"They must be at the back," Zac said to Valeria, closing the door behind him. He led Valeria through the darkened hall into the bright kitchen, but there was nobody.

"Grandma? Grandpa?" Zac called out loudly, his voice echoing through the rooms of the ground floor, but all he was greeted by was the hollow silence of the large dwelling.

"I only arrived yesterday," Zac turned to tell Valeria, who had made herself comfortable on the dinner table. "I really don't know my way around this house. They could be anywhere."

Valeria was still panting from all the running they were doing earlier. She was content just to sit down comfortably and catch her breath.

"I'll go fetch them," said Zac.

"I'll be right here," said Valeria.

Zac set off to the stairwell Grandma had used the previous night when they went looking for Grandpa.

At World's End

They're probably up there, Zac said to himself, making his way to the stairwell. *What is up there, anyway?*

Zac realized that he would eventually find out what was up there when he had climbed the rungs to the third floor. The familiar banging and crashing noises he had heard from the previous night was now audible. This time, the sounds were louder and much scarier, considering he was so close to the source.

He opened the door to the third floor from the stairwell, creeping into the darkened rooms and making his way to the door at the far end of the hallway. Upon opening the door, more darkness greeted him.

At World's End

He just realized his mistake as he walked through the door.

I haven't carried any light source, he thought to himself as he started walking down the hallway. The scratching and crashing noises were well audible now. He could stride to the door to the room from which the sounds were emanating from.

"Grandma? Grandpa?" Zac called out into the darkness, and suddenly, the crashing and scratching noises halted. It was so sudden that Zac stopped right in his tracks, just as sudden as the noises had stopped.

"Grandma? Grandpa?"

At World's End

The darkness was eerie and startling, and he could not see anything that was before him. But he knew that there was something there lurking in the darkness.

Was it not his grandparents?

He took one more step forward, then realized, to his horror, that there was something breathing very heavily right in front of him. Whoever it was, it was breathing with the kind of pants that a dog makes on a hot day.

What the hell? Zac thought to himself.

Fear was already spiraling through Zac's body, and he could not understand the shock of the situation that he was facing. It was now clear to him that his grandparents were not there.

At World's End

He turned around on the spot, and, blindly, without a second's hesitation, he took to his heels.

The door to the darkened room was only a few feet away, and he suddenly heard the alarming sounds of movement right behind him.

Oh God, he thought to himself.

He burst into the dark room, realizing that there was somebody or *something* right on his heels.

"Valeria!" He shouted, reaching the door to the stairwell. However, a strong hand grabbed his foot, with a strong vice grip that made Zac lose his balance and topple heavily to the dusty floor.

At World's End

All Zac could do at that point was to scream at the top of his lungs.

Chapter 14

Zac felt his body floating, higher and higher into the sky. He was enjoying the trance-like feeling because it made him feel calm and at peace with himself and with the white puffy clouds swooshing past him.

Then, he started to come down.

Fast.

The swooshing clouds began to climb higher and higher with increasing speed as Zac plummeted, and he felt irritated that his comfort would now have to be taken away from him. He closed his eyes in an attempt to take himself back to the trance-like feeling, but when he opened his eyes, he was back at home.

At World's End

He was standing right in the middle of the kitchen at his family's familiar squeezed house. He could not understand what he was doing there, but the sounds of shouting and screaming outside prompted him to open the tiny back door and step into the rainy street.

There were people running and screaming everywhere, with a group of people clutching their possessions trying to make it as fast as possible through the drenched streets.

Zac stood there and watched as everybody scrambled about, wondering what was causing all the mayhem in this beautiful kingdom he called home. Vandals were breaking windows, and shops were being looted.

At World's End

But what set Zac in motion through the damaged streets was the distinct clamor of conflict. He could hear people fighting in the distance, canons, and guns going off, and the clanking of swords.

There was a battle somewhere, and he needed to see what was going on. He ambled determinedly through the streets, passing a screaming child left in the middle of the road, crying with tears streaming down her beautiful face and clutching a small toy rattle in her hand.

Zac stopped there for a moment, looking at the crying little girl and wondering what she had done to deserve this fate. He threw a quick glance about him, trying to locate where the parents of the crying baby would be, but everybody around him either did not notice the crying baby or simply chose to ignore her.

Zac bent over to try and reach for the baby, but just as he did, a horses' carriage zoomed past, narrowly missing Zac's outstretched hand by inches, but managing to trample squarely over the little baby.

Even before Zac had noticed, he was suddenly drenched in blood, and that specific section of the road was swiftly given a blaring new color in the sheeting rainfall.

Nobody around him seemed to notice the abrupt tragedy—with everybody focused on their own problems.

At World's End

Zac turned and started walking slowly in the direction of the mayhem.

Zac stretched out his arms to allow the blood that had splattered all over him to drip down systematically. He did not want to think much about the incident, and so he continued slowly down the street, the rain doing its job to clean him up.

By the time he got to the lower section of the street, he watched in amazement as two groups of people fought in the valley below. In the distance, he could see the famous port that led away from the kingdom—Poseidon.

At World's End

It was the busiest freight city in the kingdom, and on this occasion, there happened to be a dozen black-painted ships anchored in its harbors.

A group of warriors from the ships were streaming onto the island, and they were magnificent black people. They were met with heavy resistance on the peripheries of the port from the familiar helmet-clad defense forces of the kingdom.

The invaders wielded all sorts of weapons, from large machetes and knives to miniature pistols and rifles. They were dressed in all-black overalls, whereas the defense forces of the kingdom were dressed in white armor. There was a desperate fight for supremacy, with both sides contesting for the control of the harbor.

At World's End

Behind the invaders, on their ships, there were large cannons supporting the invasion and blasting away any signs of civilization within range.

The invaders appeared to be achieving a superior position, causing the kingdom's defense forces to back away from the battlefield and taking full control of the port's spacious landing areas.

The invaders were shouting at the top of their lungs and inspiring their colleagues to destroy the port and kill the enemy. The kingdom's defense forces were genuinely looking overwhelmed, and Zac started to wonder where the Order of magicians was.

The heavy rainfall was not helping matters, and it made the battleground dangerously slick and slippery.

At World's End

The corpses were significant in numbers on the ground, and there was also a lot of blood everywhere that Zac could lay his eyes on.

As a youngster, he had been taught in school that the kingdom did have a defense force charged with the protection of the kingdom from foreign attackers. Additionally, he was taught that there was an Order of magicians in the kingdom, exclusively appointed by the King to act as the guardians of the kingdom.

Zac knew that Atlantis was a magical kingdom. Yet he could not understand why no magic was being used to expel what appeared to be a formidable foreign attack on the kingdom.

At World's End

Where is the Order of magicians? Zac wondered to himself, watching as the slaughter of the kingdom's defense forces peaked.

There was a loud roar of joy and exaltation from the invaders as the kingdom's defense forces started to retreat. The intensity of the battle was well against their favor, and it just so happened that this specific battleground worked to the favor of the better-prepared invaders.

As the kingdom's defense forces continued to sustain a shielded retreat, a new significant problem emerged: Large, black pipes had been thrown onto the harbor from the invaders' ships, and they were snaking through the battlefield that was already disgustingly littered with corpses.

At World's End

What Zac could not see was that the pipes were pouring a thick, black liquid onto the port, and before long, the mixture of rainwater and the dark fluid had caused it to spread almost everywhere.

Then, without warning, from nothing, the entire port started dancing and crackling in flames.

Chapter 15

The horrid unpleasantness of the fire manifested itself in screams and destruction as it swept throughout the largest port city in Atlantis. The invaders had marked a clear victory, and now they retreated back into their ships as the port was slowly consumed by the flames.

Zac watched in horror and then felt himself moving once again, moving so quickly and yet having no control of the rapid motion.

It then became apparent to him that his motion was being guided by an individual. Only when he was close behind him did he notice, to his surprise, who he was actually following.

The king's son? Zac thought to himself.

At World's End

In the middle of the city, on a narrow path preserved exclusively for the royal family, Romanus strode briskly to the King's Court.

The building before him was one of the most beautiful pieces of architecture on the island of Atlantis, and there were two guards armed with spears opening the huge mahogany doors for him.

When he had gotten up the stairs to the King's personal chambers, the door was being held open for him, and he was somewhat surprised by the sight that greeted him.

The room was dark, and the only source of illumination was a fire crackling in the middle of the room.

At World's End

"Ah, my son is finally here," boomed the flamboyant voice of Apollos, the King.

There were about fourteen people, including the King, seated around the fire. The strangest thing was that the fire seemed to be floating on its own above the concrete floor of the room. Each person around the fire was holding a large wooden mug, and there seemed to be a certain tension in the room that Romanus could not describe.

Zac was following slowly and quietly. He looked around slowly in surprise, recognizing the fact that it was his first time in this room.

"Come, join us," said Apollos, pointing to a chair next to him.

At World's End

Just as Romanus was walking across the room to take his seat, a loud banging noise surprised everybody, and it was followed by a large flash of light from outside, bright enough to illuminate the darkest corners of the room even from behind closed drapes.

Apollos burst out laughing. The other people in the room remained silent.

"That's the sign of the gods' approval, my people," Apollos said just as Romanus took his seat. Zac strode over to stand beside him.

"Approval for what?"

All the eyes in the room now turned to Rosa, all except the King who kept on laughing.

At World's End

"Ah, Rosa," said the King, interrupting his mirth by chugging his drink, "you're always too serious."

Rosa had a serious expression transfixed on her face—the black mascara on her visage was befitting to her dark mood. She got to her feet and slowly walked across the room towards the window. She opened the drapes and flung open the windows.

There was a fire raging just below the King's Court, and the sounds of screaming and disaster unexpectedly floated into the room.

"We are the King's Court, but we choose to make decisions behind closed drapes," said Rosa, with her back turned on the rest of the people in the room.

The King now frowned and put his drink down.

"Careful, Rosa," he growled.

"Now that your son is here," said Rosa, turning and walking back to her seat, "tell us why you have summoned us."

The King turned to Romanus. As Rosa took her seat, Romanus got to his feet.

"I would like to thank my father for this opportunity to speak to the Court," he said, "I am still new to the kingdom, but my life outside the island has taught me that there is still much to explore out there."

"How long have you been in Atlantis?" Came a voice from the other side of the fire. It was Lazarus'.

At World's End

"I just arrived on the island last night," he said, "but I have no regrets. I feel that my father's decision to have me raised away from Atlantis was a good decision because I am ready to save the kingdom."

"What's a boy who's never lived in Atlantis going to know about saving this glorious island?" Came another voice. It was Mila's.

Romanus turned to her.

"I have managed to gain wisdom beyond measure."

"What is that supposed to mean to the rest of us?" Came another voice. It was Octavia's.

Romanus turned to her. "The defense of the kingdom is in my foremost priority, and despite what some of you might know or not know about me, I intend to secure the assistance of every member of the Order for the successful defense of the kingdom."

There was an ominous silence hanging in the room. Zac could tell that they were all nervous about speaking their minds, particularly in the presence of the King.

"I think that's settled, then," said the King in his booming voice. "My son will use all your help in defense of the kingdom. Give him your support, all of you. He will lead the kingdom's defense."

The King pushed himself to his feet and slowly shuffled to the door, a big smile still plastered on his face while clutching his large wooden cup. Everybody in the room bowed their heads as he shuffled for the door, and once the door behind him had been banged shut, everybody in the room started talking all at once.

Romanus remained standing next to his seat, watching as everybody chattered and took to their wooden cups.

Suddenly, Rosa shot to her feet, commanding the attention of everybody in the room. Romanus' eyes appeared to narrow down as he looked at Rosa, who had managed to shut everybody up.

"You're a very lucky young boy," she said, pointing directly at Romanus with her half-empty cup. "You get to live."

At World's End

"Careful, Rosa," said Octavius, motioning to Rosa to sit down. "He's still the King's son."

Rosa had a big frown on her face. "I guess that makes you lucky, then," she said, addressing Romanus. "I can't figure out why the rest of us must remain so cool, yet your father has murdered all our sons."

Romanus did not say anything, instead choosing to remain silent. The room was now deathly quiet, with the only sounds floating into the room being of those from the decimated kingdom.

"Just to let you know," said Rosa, coldly, with Zac watching in amazement from Romanus' side. "If you don't successfully defend the kingdom, I'll sacrifice you to the gods myself."

Chapter 16

There was a haze of darkness that was interspersed with moments of distant shouting and moments of freezing cold. However, Zac could not tell exactly where he was until a bright flash of light jarred him back to what he assumed was the reality.

Before him, a great battle was raging. Unlike the battle earlier in the port of Poseidon, he noticed that this was a comprehensive battle that involved both the defending forces of the kingdom alongside the Order of the magicians.

The scene was truly amazing and impressive for Zac.

In the sky, a group of ten men and women floated about, aiming their wands strategically into the battlefield. Above them, dark rain clouds hovered about, declaring their intent with the menacing lightning and thunderstorms illuminating different sections of the charcoal sky.

Below them, there was a full-scale clash between the defense forces and the invading forces, and the battle truly looked horrific. The highest sections of the battle were fought on top of a mountain of dead corpses, and the surrounding buildings and structures that once made up the capital city of Poseidon had all been leveled.

There was thick glutinous smoke hovering over the fighters and an acrid smell that was a mixture of blood, sweat, and gunpowder rent the air. There was horrendous screaming everywhere, and this time, the battle tide seemed to be in favor of the defenders.

They fought off the invaders valiantly who clearly had a firepower and moral advantage. They were well prepared for the war, using their ships anchored in the waters to control the port town and offer support to the fighters on land.

From where Zac was, he could see that a significant section of the kingdom seemed to be on fire. The once peaceful and beautiful home that he had left under mysterious circumstances only a few hours ago seemed to be falling apart entirely.

Then, in the midst of the battle, he saw a sight that surprised and relieved him at the same time.

At World's End

Up in the sky, linking up with the other Order magicians who were waging war on the defenders, Zac saw his father and Dolores, pointing their wands down below and joining the fight.

Zac called out to his father but realized that his voice was not audible, even to himself. He attempted to shout and scream in his father's direction, but he stopped, grasping that his efforts truly were in vain.

The invaders were getting pushed back, and they seemed incapable of mounting a stern resistance against the defenders who were backed by the Order magicians from above.

Then, Zac saw the strangest thing. The Order magicians, who, for the most part, were fighting from the sky, pulled back their wands and started flying away into the distance, progressively disappearing from the sky above the battlefield. Zac saw that his father was among the last Order magicians to disappear from the battle scene.

Then, the heavens opened—at first small, unnoticeable raindrops, to an outright outpour. The dark clouds above the battlefield that were threatening to wet the fighters had finally fulfilled its menace.

Within minutes, the whole battlefield was awash with mud and puddles everywhere, with the invaders being dealt a blow. They were pushed back onto their ships, and the defenders of the island roared in the glee of their victory.

However, Zac felt that their happiness would be short-lived because the invaders had lost a fight but had not lost the war.

Zac started to move in the direction that he saw his father disappearing to, but his movements now seemed inhibited, and he could hear the constant din of somebody calling out to him. He could not understand what he was doing in Atlantis, back at home, but when he closed his eyes, he felt like he was going down a water slide that seemed to have no end.

"Zac–Zac," there was a constant voice in the back of his head, and he tried paying more attention to it. "Zac! Wake up–can you hear me?"

At World's End

When Zac opened his eyes, he saw the face of Valeria over him, staring into his eyes with a pained concern.

"Zac–are you okay?" She asked. "Are you with me?"

Zac tried to raise his head, but there was a knocking pain at the back of his head that made him lie back down immediately.

"Ow," he exclaimed, clutching the back of his head.

"Sorry about that," said Valeria, prying the back of his head to see that he was okay. "The side-effects of my magic."

Zac threw a glance around him, noticing that he was in the living room of his grandparent's house. There were worn and old couches everywhere, and there were sets of unique furniture adorning the room that Zac had never seen before in his life. The floor was heavily carpeted in a thick, green and woolly rug, and there were strange portraits on the walls of people that Zac did not know. There were heavy awning green drapes to match the carpet concealing the snowstorm that was raging beyond the windows.

"Where are my grandparents?" Zac asked Valeria, who was still standing over him. The concerned expression had not left her face, and she was observing Zac's reactions intently.

"Your grandparents haven't returned," she said. "I don't know where they are."

Zac frowned. "What happened to me?"

At World's End

Valeria also frowned. "Don't you remember?"

"I remember something in that hallway upstairs, something that grabbed my leg," said Zac. "Then I was back home. What happened?"

Valeria sighed loudly, rolling her eyes. She got to her feet and disappeared into the next room for a few minutes, re-emerging clutching two steaming white ceramic cups. She handed one of them to Zac.

"There's something strange going on here," said Valeria, kneeling on the carpet next to Zac while clutching her cup in both hands and taking a meticulous sip. "I'm not sure how to break this down for you or if you'll believe me in the first place."

At World's End

"Tell me what happened to me from the moment that thing grabbed my leg," demanded Zac.

"Well," said Valeria, "I used my wand to teleport your body away from here. The teleportation only lasts a few hours."

"You can do magic? How come? In my kingdom, nobody is taught to use magic until the age of eighteen," Zac complained.

"I can do magic, and I teleported you to the one place that you want to be," said Valeria. "Home."

Zac could still feel himself hovering in Atlantis, watching over the battles that would determine the fate of his home.

"What was that thing?" Zac asked, remembering the stronghold that had his leg before he was teleported. "What was that?"

"That was a monster," Valeria said plainly.

"Was it the same as the one you showed me earlier?" Zac sounded astounded. "Was it at the edge of the world, you said?"

"You don't believe it was the edge of the world?" Valeria asked.

"I know that we live on a globe," said Zac, "How can that be possible? And monsters—what the hell is going on in this place?"

"I think your grandparents are keeping monsters in the upper floors of this house," said Valeria.

Zac frowned. "That would explain the strange sounds I've heard ever since I got here."

"But if I'm going to be even more honest with you," said Valeria, "I'm not exactly a resident of this place. I moved here a couple of years ago."

Zac raised his eyes to look at her blue eyes.

"I was in a similar situation just like you," said Valeria. "My home was destroyed, and my entire family was murdered—but by virtue of being here, I managed to survive."

Zac's eyes widened. "What are you trying to say?"

At World's End

"The moment you got to this place, Zac," said

Valeria, "is the moment that you started a new life

because there is no going back."

Chapter 17

Outside the farmhouse, darkness was starting to set in once more. The icy sheeting winds were accompanied by heavy snowing that added thicker layers of snow on the already-cramped ground.

Inside the house, Zac and Valeria huddled closer to each other for warmth. It did not occur to either of them that a fire could be lit in the large, old-fashioned fireplace at the far end of the room.

"What are we going to do?" Zac asked. "I must get back home; I must make sure that my father is safe."

Valeria gave him a half smile. "It won't be possible to leave this place now that you are here," she said. "Your own grandparents won't allow it."

At World's End

"Why not?" Zac asked. He seemed puzzled by the suggestion. "As far as I'm concerned, I'm a guest intruding on their space."

Valeria smiled wryly. "Your grandparents might not be the innocent people that you think they are."

"I'm starting to get an idea," said Zac, looking at the ceiling of the living room. "You say that there are monsters living in the upper section of this house? How is that possible?"

Valeria looked deeply into Zac's black eyes. "I can tell you the full truth—if you want," she said.

She got to her feet and picked up her wand that was on top of the table. She flickered it slightly, and a big, black book appeared out of thin air right on top of the table above where the wand was positioned.

"This is an important book," said Valeria. "It is the thousand-history volume of this place. It's available at the local library."

"There is a local library?" Zac asked. "Where are all these places?"

"Everything is right here on the South Pole," said Valeria. She skimmed through the pages of the thick black book, looking for a specific chapter, then put her hand to her lips to silence any questions from Zac.

At World's End

"Let me read this to you," she said, her index finger keeping track of a definite part of the page. "This will answer all your questions."

She coughed a little to clear her throat—then she began to quote:

"In the beginning, the land was inhabited by beasts and the most majestic creatures allowed by the gods to tread this land. The land was a paradise; there were no controls other than those enforced by nature, and all the animals could find peaceful coordination in the land. Then came the human beings. The most important part of human history, and perhaps the only important truth about where human beings came from can be answered in the Land of Ice. Very deceptively, in the future, this same region of the world will come to be known as the 'South Pole.'"

Valeria paused for a moment, noticing that Zac had a big frown on his face. His mouth was already bubbling with questions, and his eyes widened as though he had seen something that Valeria had not.

"Just remain silent and listen," she said before Zac could speak up, "I've barely read anything yet. This passage has all the answers to the questions I'm sure you're about to ask me. Be patient and listen."

"What kind of history is that?" Zac asked when he finally found his words.

Valeria replaced the serious look on her face with a smile.

"Just be patient and listen," she said. "This passage will offer an explanation to everything."

At World's End

Zac maintained a skeptical silence as Valeria sought the specific section in the book she had left off. Then she resumed:

"The Land of Ice was the first human discovery of the Earth, and the first of them to make it that far from the rest of the universe fulfilled an ancient prophecy that human beings would finally get to the center of the universe. Many of those early humans settled in these icy lands, assuming that the Land of Ice was the actual center of the universe. However, not all land was ice in the Land of Ice, and there were significant sections for cultivation and other important survival activities. However, the coldness in this section of the Earth was demoralizing, and many humans migrated inland, building simple but sophisticated ships at the beginning that allowed them to spread to the rest of the world.

At World's End

But war was to come—the first significant conflict among human beings in the center of the universe. For those who migrated into the Earth from the Land of Ice, they set up their own kingdoms and their own zones of control, thereby disrupting a peaceful cycle of nature that had existed before their arrival. Worse still, the humans who had migrated into the center of the universe denounced the first settlers in the Land of Ice and any connection they had to them."

A loud crash from the upper floors above interrupted Valeria's soft voice. Valeria looked up from her book, staring at Zac. Then, a second crashing noise, this time louder, and the evident sound of shuffling feet could be heard.

Zac had a pained look on his face. "The monsters?"

Valeria nodded.

"I would like to get out of here," Zac said, "perhaps to your place? But I need to wait for my grandparents."

Valeria remained silent for a moment.

"How many monsters are up there?" He asked.

"Probably hundreds," said Valeria. "Who knows?"

"I don't get it," said Zac. "Why would my grandparents be living here with monsters?"

Valeria started to reply, but just as she was opening her mouth, a large shadow suddenly appeared at the doorway of the living room. The door was some distance from where Valeria and Zac were huddled up, but the shadow was so long it managed to get to them.

"Grandma? Grandpa?" Zac called out but immediately comprehended his error.

The familiar sound of heavy breathing and grunting that he had heard on his first night when he ascended to the third floor via the rickety staircases with his grandmother was audible.

Zac immediately bolted to his feet.

But it was too late to go anywhere.

A large, green-skinned, yellow-eyed monster sauntered casually into the room.

Chapter 18

Zac immediately scrambled behind Valeria, who unflinchingly got to her feet. The big book fell to the carpeted floor in a heap, and Valeria was clutching her wand steadily in her right hand.

The monster let out a disgusting growl, and upon closer inspection, Zac noticed that it was oozing a slimy fluid all over its body, leaving a smarmy trail in its wake.

It opened its mouth, still moving forward towards Zac and Valeria, revealing a rotting set of yellowed teeth and thick, glutinous saliva dribbling from its hippo-like mouth.

At World's End

It let out a loud roar, a familiar bellow like the one Zac had heard earlier from the even bigger monster that had attempted to confront him and Valeria earlier on at the edge.

"Let's get out of here!" Zac said, starting to turn around to run in the opposite direction, but was surprised that Valeria did not flinch or move in the slightest.

Instead, she took aim with her wand at the monster, and closed her eyes, chanting something to herself that was inaudible to Zac. The monster had closed in on Valeria, who was still standing calmly at the same spot.

At World's End

Zac closed his eyes, realizing that they were done for as there was nowhere to run nor anywhere to hide. He could not believe that his end had come in such a gruesome manner.

Then, abruptly, there was a very bright flash of light, so bright that it was visible despite Zac's closed eyes.

"Hey!" He shouted in surprise. There was an equally loud sound to accompany the bright flash of light— the sound of thunder, and when Zac lifted his hands from his eyes, he realized that he was standing alone in the room with Valeria.

What had just happened?

He looked around, realizing that whatever had transpired had only lasted a few microseconds. There was no sign of a monster or any other presence near them.

"W-what did you do?" Zac asked, his voice bordering on hysteria.

"I zapped it away," Valeria said, calmly. She had not moved from the same spot that she was standing, and her wand was still pointed in front of her at the exact spot that the monster had been.

"We'll have to get out of here," Valeria said.

"I can't," he replied, "I have to wait for my grandparents. I have no idea where they are."

Valeria turned to face him, placing her wand back on the table.

At World's End

"I'll remain here with you, then," she said, "I can wait here for your grandparents with you."

Zac nodded. "I appreciate that. But I must ask: Where are the monsters coming from?"

Valeria returned to where she was sitting, retrieved the big black book from the floor and motioned for Zac to take a seat as well.

"I'll read it for you," she said.

When Zac was settled beside her, Valeria flipped through the pages of the book until she got to where she had been cut off earlier by the monster. Then, she resumed reading;

At World's End

"War broke out, the first ever recorded full-scale conflict between two groups of human beings. This only caused the human population to migrate even further throughout the world, thereby occupying every piece of land that was around the center of the universe, commonly referred to as the 'North Pole'. The battle that was raging never ended per se, but it remained manifested in different types of conflicts that exist throughout history to the present days. The objective of the original dwellers of the Land of Ice was to enhance the togetherness of the human community. The wars ensured that the dwellers of the Land of Ice were isolated and forgotten about, and they decided to leave the center of the universe and wander back into the darkness. Many of them simply turned around and returned to where they came from, but there was a large community that remained in the Land of Ice.

At World's End

For those who returned to the universe, they brought word with them that they had indeed found the center of the universe. Seven kings of the universe mounted a collective effort to organize a large force that would come to the center of the universe and take over the Earth. However, this attack would never materialize because, just as the armies were reaching the edge of the Earth, they noticed that the land was being protected by several large animals roaming in the exterior, and a very large ice wall had been constructed, so high it was touching the clouds.

'Who could have done this? Who could have erected this barrier?' The seven kings would ask, but they soon got their reply. A tall-looking man with wings sprouting from his back would swoop from the skies towards the seven kings and their armies. He told them:

At World's End

The Earth is the kingdom of the gods, and all her children that are dwelling there will not be harmed by any outsiders. The gods have named the center of the universe "The Garden of Eden," and only the human beings living within its constraints would determine its destiny.'

The kings ignored this strange person, choosing to attack the barrier instead, but with all their firepower, they could not get past the large ice wall. Then, they had to face the strongest enemy of them all—green, slimy monsters in numerous numbers kept attacking the kings' camps and slaughtered a great large number of people through the nights. They were mainly nocturnal creatures, and they swept through the camps, killing in a bestial fashion, and feasting on the flesh of some of their victims. Within a few days since setting off to conquer the center of the universe, the kings had lost well over half of their armies, and it was at that point that they conceded defeat and turned

back, never to return again."

Valeria looked up from her book to be greeted by a skeptical look on Zac's face.

"So, what do the monsters have to do with my grandparents?" He asked.

Valeria sighed. "I'm not going to claim I know anything, but I believe that the monster story as it is told in this official book is propaganda."

Zac raised his eyebrows.

"In my time here," Valeria said, "I have come to know that monsters are created by magic. So, the seven kings who were repelled by the monsters were not defeated by a supernatural being, but by the work of the people who were living in the Land of Ice."

Zac now frowned.

"So," resumed Valeria, "I believe that your grandparents' ancestors might have been the very people who created the monsters."

Chapter 19

"Where are my grandparents, then?" Zac asked. The story that Valeria had read to him had only made him more anxious, and he still could not fathom exactly what he was supposed to be believing.

Valeria shook her head.

"We need to go out there and look for them, then," Zac said.

"And then what?" Valeria asked. "What are you going to do, then?"

"I have to go back home," said Zac, "I don't care if there's a war. I doubt I'll be any safer here."

At World's End

"Didn't you see what was happening back in Atlantis when I teleported you earlier?" Valeria asked. She had a concerned look on her face.

"Aren't you seeing what's happening here?" Zac retorted.

"Look," said Valeria, lifting both her hands up. "At this hour, there's only one place they can be. The local synagogue."

"Take me there," demanded Zac. "It doesn't seem like they'll be back any time soon."

Valeria sighed. "We'll be safer here."

"I don't think we're safe anywhere, Valeria," said Zac. He got to his feet and disappeared out of the room for a few minutes, leaving Valeria to make the large,

black book disappear once more with a wave of her

wand. When Zac returned, he was clad in a different

large, grey, woolly jacket.

He was extra prepared for the cold that was outside.

Zac walked to the hallway and pulled open the front

door, Valeria following timidly.

The snow outside seemed to be falling faster in the

night than in the day. Despite the darkness that had

spread through the land, Zac could see that it seemed

to be twice as cold and the winds were visibly swirling

snow into the air.

"No way my grandparents are coming back with this kind of snow," said Zac. "We best go to—where did you say? The synagogue?"

Zac turned to look at Valeria, who nodded. She was also pulling a heavy black coat around her, one that Zac had not seen before.

"The synagogue is that way," said Valeria, pointing.

They stepped out into the freezing ground, Zac shutting the door to the house behind them, and they slowly set off into the cold winds. Unlike daytime, Zac could now see even less of the surrounding landscape. He was surprised by how quickly the night had already set in, but the most surprising of the weird events was that, for the entire day, he had gone without seeing his grandparents.

Could they be worshipping in the synagogue all this time? He asked himself.

"What's a synagogue doing here in the South Pole?" He directed his question at Valeria. "Do you believe in the same gods that we do?"

"Of course," replied Valeria.

They walked on for what seemed an eternity to Zac before they started spotting signs of life.

"The synagogue's up ahead," said Valeria, pulling her coat tighter around her. Her visage had paled from the cold, and she could not control the chattering of her teeth.

When Zac squinted through the snow to see more clearly of what was ahead of them, he was flabbergasted beyond measure.

"Where's the synagogue?" Zac asked.

"We'll have to get past those," said Valeria, motioning with her head.

Zac confirmed his worst fears when they got close enough. Before them lay a long stretch of graves, and in the distance, Zac saw a section of the ground that seemed to be covered exclusively by red and black tiles.

At World's End

"The synagogue is underground," said Valeria, looking at Zac and reading his questions from his puzzled face.

"W-what about the graveyard?" Zac asked—he had a slight tremble in his voice. "Who are all these people buried here?"

There was a strong wind blowing through the place, and it was accompanied by a strange howl that made Zac look about him nervously.

"This is where everybody who dies in the South Pole is buried," said Valeria. "It's a very sacred site."

"Next to an underground synagogue?" Zac's response was both a question and a statement of fact.

At World's End

"Come on," said Valeria, motioning with her head. "This way."

She set off on a path that was built through the middle of the cemetery. The tombstones were like eerie cylindrical stone tablets reaching out for air from the thick snow cover. From where Zac was, he could see that the tombstones were engraved with different markings, but he could not seem to understand what language they were inscribed in.

"Valeria," He shouted, "what language is this?"

He had not noticed that Valeria had gone a step further than him, far enough from earshot.

Zac knelt beside the first tombstone he encountered, clutching his jacket as a burst of wind blew snow and icy coldness through the place. The engraving seemed to be in strange shapes and letters that Zac did not recognize.

When he looked up, Valeria had disappeared into the swirling winds.

"Valeria!" He shouted, standing up and looking around him. Valeria was nowhere in sight.

Maybe she's got to the synagogue, he thought to himself, wondering how she could have vanished so abruptly. He told himself that he would find out more about the strange markings on the tombstones. They were truly strange and unconventional for Zac.

The graveyard was very creepy and certainly did not look like a place that would be harboring a synagogue so close by. The strong winds gusting through the place were kicking up so much snow into the air—it was almost impossible for Zac to see what was up ahead.

No wonder Valeria had managed to disappear.

Zac stumbled through the snow, past the bulging tombstones to the tiled section of the ground. But as he got there, he heard a bone-chilling sound that he hoped he would never have to hear ever again.

Oh no, he said to himself, *not out here in the open!*

He turned around.

Out in the open snow, in the howling wind, in the moonlit twilight, danger lurked.

At World's End

Zac was very familiar with the sounds that were approaching him through the haze.

The evident howling and panting of the barking ghosts.

Chapter 20

Where's Valeria? Zac asked himself, turning around on the spot and scrambling towards a descending section of the cemetery beneath the tiled section on the ground.

As he scrambled downwards, he noticed that, on the ground before him, Valeria's familiar wand lay waiting to be picked up.

The sounds of the approaching beasts were getting closer, and so Zac instinctively picked up the wand and scrambled further down the dirt.

A wooden door that was ajar and seemed to be leading to some sort of underground basement came into sight.

At World's End

"Valeria!" Zac called out, reaching the door, entering inside a large, dark hollow room, and closing the door shut behind him. He realized that he was panting hard, and despite the cold, he was sweating.

"What the hell is wrong with this place?" He asked himself aloud in the darkness. His life in the past few days was akin to the type of intriguing experiences that he only heard of in stories.

He stood there holding the door shut for a second to catch his breath—then, he called out:

"Valeria? Are you in here?"

His voice bounced off the walls of the darkened underground space, and there was nothing but silence to greet him.

At World's End

Is Valeria still outside? He asked himself.

And then he heard it.

A bone-chilling scream that made the insides of his stomach turn inside-out.

It was Valeria.

She was screaming at the top of her lungs, frantically as though she was fighting off something.

Oh my God, Zac realized, starting to pull open the door. *I have her wand. She can't defend herself.*

The screams were loud and desperate, and Zac was not entirely sure of what he was supposed to do. But there was no way that he was going to leave Valeria out there with the barking ghosts.

At World's End

Then, he heard a stern and strong voice somewhere behind him instructing him:

"Don't open the door."

Zac froze like the snowy ground outside. He felt a tingling sensation traversing the length of his spine.

"W-who's there?" He asked in a frightened, shaky voice. He did not turn around, and he was realizing for the first time that he was not alone in the darkness.

There was no response from the darkness.

The screams from outside seemed to be subsiding. Zac's heart was beating very fast, and the sweating seemed to go on unabated. His hand was still strongly clutching the side of the door.

He let go rather hesitantly.

In his other hand, he flicked the wand he was holding, more in fear rather than knowledge of what he was doing, and a faint light appeared at the tip of the wand.

The screams from outside had now subsided, and Zac turned around, walked into the darkness, holding the wand before him. Just as he was squinting into the blackness, trying to get a focus on who might be before him by using the faint light from the top of the wand, there was a loud whooshing sound, and a large fire sprung out of the darkness to consume the darkness in an instant.

"Whoa!" Zac screeched, startled, and was thrown a step backward.

The fire had instantaneously appeared out of nowhere, and it burned around a perfect circular pit dug shallowly into the ground.

The fire, however, allowed Zac to see the depths of the large room, finally.

There were long wooden benches before him that crossed the entire length of the room to the very back. He was standing on what appeared to be a pew, and the fireplace before him was right in front of the first benches.

At World's End

And on them, there were about ten hooded figures with their hands clamped together in prayer. Their heads were bowed very low, and they all wore long black hoods that completely concealed their faces and any details about their bodies.

The only sound in the room was the crackling of the flames, and Zac stood rooted for a moment in the same spot wondering what he was supposed to be doing.

Then, one of the hooded figures raised his head, but Zac was still unable to see the face concealed in the darkness created by the hood. The individual stood up, with the others still in prayer, the invisible face of the individual trained squarely on Zac.

At World's End

"W-who are you?" Zac finally got the courage to force out words from his mouth.

The hooded figure did not reply. Instead, he walked slowly towards Zac, his eyes trained on the youngster the entire time. He walked with a slow amble and a purposeful spring in his footsteps.

And then he did the most remarkable thing.

He walked through the flaming fire in the middle of the room, throwing Zac's mouth agape. He walked calmly and composed through the fire, never taking a glance away from Zac.

The room darkened slightly as the figure walked through the fire, and in a moment, he was standing right in front of Zac.

At World's End

Zac could smell a burnt rubber odor as the figure stood in front of him, silently watching him. However, neither his apparels nor his body was on fire, nor was he scathed with the scorching heat in any way.

Zac took a step back and pointed the wand at the figure.

"Who are you?" Zac demanded. "I'm looking for my grandparents. Have you seen them?"

His words echoed off the darkened walls, and he could not control his sweating. His nervousness took precedence over any aspect of normalcy he might have tried to muster.

At World's End

Realizing that he had no idea of what was going on and the probability of Valeria laying dead outside, he decided to throw caution to the wind.

Surprising the hooded figure, Zac turned around, and without hesitation, scrambled for the door despite the danger of the looming barking ghosts outside.

He yanked open the door just as he heard disgruntled sounds behind him. A burst of cold icy air hit him, and without looking back, he set off into the snow once more.

Chapter 21

"Valeria! Where are you? Valeria!"

Zac was running at full speed, his sneakers squishing the spongy, white ground. He ascended from the descent of the ground in the cemetery, and he was suddenly confronted with a shocking sight before him.

Leaning on the bottom trunk of a large tree in the middle of the cemetery, Valeria lay there, bloodied, and a significant chunk of her lustrous hair ripped from her forehead. It was the type of scene that Zac would have expected of the war zone back at home, but the sight of his newfound friend had a chilling impact on him.

At World's End

Without thinking, and without looking around to see if the barking ghosts might still be there, he dashed towards Valeria, zigzagging past the creepy tombstones and stumbling twice into the deep snow.

"Valeria!" He could not keep her name out of his mouth.

When he got to her, Valeria was clutching her chest, with a stream of blood gushing through her hands. Her eyes were only opened half-way, and she had multiple cuts and bruises all over her skin.

Her top and jacket were already soaked in blood, and they were already taking to the new color change with dramatic effect. Valeria was panting hard, trying to suck in all the air around her.

At World's End

She raised her eyes very exhaustedly at Zac whose face was printed with nothing but concern. His eyes were full of pity, and he was struggling to fight back the tears.

"Valeria," he said softly, leaning down beside her, and flicking her hair. He was too afraid to try and assess her evident fatal injuries.

"I-I'm so sorry," she whispered to Zac, blood spluttering from her mouth. She coughed heavily, seething in pain as more blood gushed from the open wound on her chest.

"What the hell are you apologizing for?" Zac asked.

At World's End

"For not being honest with you," she said weakly, coughing some more. She had no control of the blood that was evidently eager to leave her body.

"What are you talking about?" Zac asked.

"E-everything," she stammered.

"I need to get you out of here," Zac said.

Valeria seemed too injured to speak any more. She was in a lot of pain, and so Zac lifted her gingerly and started carrying her towards the cemetery's periphery.

The wind seemed to be blowing even stronger, but the snowfall appeared to have eased up. Valeria weighed a ton, and Zac was almost certain that he would not be able to carry her any further distance.

At World's End

He knew for a fact that they would not be safe in the synagogue–it was too creepy a place to be in.

But Zac needed answers.

Where were his grandparents?

Were they among the hooded figures in the synagogue?

What truths was Valeria talking about?

But more importantly, where were they going?

A strong blast of arctic wind hit Zac in the face—it was now blowing so strong that Zac could not see ahead where they were supposed to be going. The strain of carrying Valeria was quite burdensome, but he did not want to go back to the cemetery. He had already seen enough to convince himself to leave the South Pole.

The walk back to the farmhouse was an ordeal for Zac. He carried Valeria half the distance while he dragged her on the snow for the other half. The icy winds hit him relentlessly, and he thought that they would eventually consume him and Valeria. He could not see where he was going, and he could not see where he had come from. He was surprised that nobody from the synagogue had followed them and made any attempts to get to them.

When Zac finally got to the front porch of the small farmhouse, he felt a big wave of relief, but he had to stumble in first and carry Valeria all the way to the living room.

At World's End

Her eyes were firmly shut and she was barely moving. She seemed to be breathing, but only in the slightest. The blood had stopped oozing so quickly from her wound. Her arms lay limp on her side, and the full ferocity of the attack on her life was evident for Zac to see. She was paler than a ghost, and the coldness outside seemed to have had a greater effect on her than on Zac.

Zac was also pale from the cold, and he could not feel his own face when he touched himself.

He had no idea of how to conduct first aid, but he assumed that using Valeria's wand might have some effect. The wand was stashed in his pocket with its pointy end sticking out of Zac's side.

At World's End

He observed the long, black stick for a moment, noticing that the wand was made from a material that Zac had never seen before because it was not wooden per se.

Zac looked at Valeria's motionless body, wondering what he was supposed to do for her sake. However, he did not have to wonder so much as a loud crash from the upper floors above stirred him.

He did not have much time to respond because immediately he was set upon by invisible, panting beasts that surrounded the living room in an instant. They poured in from the back door, and the room was suddenly lively.

The barking ghosts, Zac told himself.

At World's End

He felt almost too exhausted to be frightened. But just as he thought the scene unfolding before him was strange, it got even stranger.

First, a green-skinned monster walked into the living room from the front door—then, another walked in from the back door. Suddenly, a dozen monsters appeared, walking in through the respective doors to the living room and standing in a ring shape around the living room.

They stood abreast the drapes, in the shadows, so that all Zac could view were their imposing yellow eyes that seemed to have live worms crawling inside them.

Zac watched in horror, mouth wide like an opened boot-lid as the monsters made sickening, excited sounds alongside the invisible beasts. They encircled Zac and the limp Valeria, their ghastly eyes excitedly settling on their prey.

Zac remained rooted to the spot, looking about him nervously, wondering how he could escape his predicament.

Then, one of the monsters stepped forward. Its skin was slimy, and his fingers had sharp, claw-like nails. It held its hands together as if in silent, demonic prayer.

"We're glad to finally meet you, Zac," it said in a growling voice. "We have so much to talk about."

Chapter 22

There was a frosty atmosphere inside the living room of the small farmhouse, far icier than the biggest storms that have ever hit the South Pole.

Zac stared into the creepy, yellowy eyes of the monster standing so close to him.

He had no idea that monsters could speak.

"W-who are you?" Zac could only stammer out his sentences. He felt that remaining motionless might help him stay alive longer.

The creepy monster that had spoken up stepped even closer to Zac. It rolled its eyes to look at Valeria, who was now set on the couch and seemed to be somewhere peaceful.

A slimy ooze was creeping down its body, and it was aptly absorbed by the thick carpet.

"We are the Guardians of the World," said the monster, still eyeing Zac with its wormy eyes. "You are the first person from the outside world that we have been able to speak to in a thousand years."

Zac remained stock-still and silent. He still could not fathom how the monster was speaking so coherently and direct.

"We are genuinely honored to meet you," it said, as a general sound of consensus spread around the room.

At World's End

Zac still could not assemble the courage to enable him to speak. He was attending the devil's assembly.

"It is a good thing that we meet now," continued the monster. "And it's because it's a chance for both of us to save our lives."

The monster inched further forward, its slimy skin coming within inches of Zac. He could smell the horrid odor of decaying mold, a swamp-like odor that seemed to follow the monster like a shadow.

"You have to realize that we will cause no harm to you," said the monster, stopping right on the edge of the couch.

Up close, Zac could see that the creature had the physique of a man, but there seemed to be something

At World's End

distorted about its body shape. Its pale, green skin was even more callous to look at up-close, and Zac was particularly revolted by its yellow teeth that had all manner of items stuck in between them, from grass clippings to chunks of meat.

"W-what are you?" Zac finally stammered after a strange silence hung in the air for a minute. The resonances of the sleeting snow and the howling wind outside interspersed the space between Zac finally uttering horrifying words, and the monster speaking.

The monster seemed to be amused by Zac's question, first staring around the room at his fellow creatures, before answering anyway:

At World's End

"I've just told you," it said, "we are the Guardians of the World."

Zac stared on as the monster continued:

"The world that you live in is full of lies; any history that you think you know is false, and the truth is the truth."

The acrid smell of decaying flesh seemed to hit Zac squarely in the face, but he did not express his disgust openly.

"W-what are you trying to tell me?" Zac had noticed that the barking ghosts seemed to have settled down on the carpet; they barely made any noise other than an occasional whimper.

At World's End

"We are the original settlers of the world," the monster spoke up, its gruff voice frightening Zac despite its assurance that the monsters will do him no harm. "The evil human beings that first inhabited the Earth were magicians. They set a spell upon us that so strong that it changed us from men into whatever you want to call this."

It gestured at itself, pointing to the fact that it had green skin covering it.

Zac had listened to so many strange things since he arrived on the South Pole; he was not interested in making any sense of what he was being told. However, he was interested in the invisible beasts.

"How would you explain the invisible animals?" He asked.

"They, too," said the monster, swaying his hand behind him to gesture at the invisible mutts, "were set upon a curse. They are to roam the Lands of Ice as invisible creatures for eternity."

"I'm sorry," said Zac, timidly. "But none of this makes any sense to me. If you're going to cause no harm to me, then can I ask you to tend to my injured friend?"

The monster's eyes switched their focus back on Valeria, and it let out a low, angry growl beneath its breath. There was some murmuring among the monsters, but Zac could not understand any of the words they were speaking at that time.

Then, the lead monster spoke up once more, "It's her and her people that are responsible for our demise, they are the real monsters."

Zac raised his eyes without asking any questions, but the monsters could see the queries plastered all over his face. There was some more murmuring going around the room.

"Your friend there and her people are magicians who came from another world that is renowned for very ugly creatures," said the monster. "When they came to this world, they turned us, the appointed

At World's End

Guardians of the World, into monsters so that they could take control."

When Zac turned to look at Valeria, wondering what sense he was making, he noticed that she had stirred and her eyes were opening slowly.

Her vision came into focus progressively, and the room hushed.

"Valeria," said Zac, sinking to the couch to embrace her. "I'm glad you're alive."

However, as he embraced her and knelt over the couch, wrapping his arms around her bloody clothes, he felt a tingling sensation on his chest, at first, then a sudden piercing pain.

At World's End

"Ow," he cried out, releasing his hold on Valeria. Then, he noticed what was happening, much to his shock.

There were long spines growing out of Valeria's body, glistened by her blood, and they were similar to that of a porcupine. They were growing slowly and purposefully while Valeria laid there, motionless with her eyes opened.

Then, her eyes also started changing from their deep blue color into a dark, hazy color that completely changed her outward appearance.

Her face seemed to collapse into itself, and all that was left was an ugly skull—her long lustrous hair disappearing as if consumed by the couch.

At World's End

Zac stared in horror, completely unable to say anything.

"You want the truth," the monster said slowly. "Here it is."

Chapter 23

The room had fallen into a dead silence as the strange transformation of Valeria continued. She transformed into something that Zac had never seen before—some type of ancient creature that he might have seen in a cult book, perhaps—some type of phoenix.

Outside, there was a snowstorm that seemed relentless on reducing the entire place into a white, sub-zero desert.

Inside, particularly inside Zac's brain, there was a storm of his own brewing, and the questions he wanted to be answered would need a lifetime to be reviewed in their entirety.

At World's End

The creature opened its eyes only once, looking straight at Zac.

It uttered in a very restrained and chocking voice; "I'm very, very sorry, Zac."

When it closed its eyes, it had taken its last breath.

There was an ominous silence that hung in the room for a while as Zac attempted to make sense of what he had just seen. However, the lead monster spoke up, breaking the silence.

"We have been in their clutches for over a thousand years," it said. "And it has given them the opportunity to spread lies for a very long time."

"Is this some sort of magic?" Zac asked quietly.

At World's End

Zac took his eyes away from the creature that now lay still on the couch and turned his attention to the problem that he resented the most—he was well and truly alone.

"We need your help," continued the monster. "We believe that you can help to reverse the spell cast upon us. Only by revealing the truth, does the truth manifest in the eyes."

The monster gestured to the creature that was once Valeria by rolling its round eyes in her general direction.

"W-what do you want me to do?" All Zac could do at that point was to stammer and try to stay alive.

At World's End

There was murmuring around the room and some loud whimpers from the barking ghosts.

Then, the lead monster spoke up once more, "The wand that you possess, do you know how to use it?"

Zac felt the pace of his heart quicken.

"No, I don't know how," he said, shaking his head fearfully. "Honestly, I have no idea how these things work or –"

"That's okay," said the monster, cutting him short, "we know that children of today do not know how to use magic. The establishment is trying to phase it out of mainstream society—even here in the South Pole."

At World's End

There was some more murmuring amongst the monsters.

"Do you know where my grandparents are?" Zac asked.

His question appeared to have touched the wrong nerve because, suddenly, the room fell silent, and stone-cold, hard eyes started staring at him. The lead monster spoke up:

"Your grandparents are responsible for holding us captive in this place," it said. "They are responsible for causing some much trouble for us."

Zac's heart was pacing.

"What did you do to them?"

At World's End

The monster raised its massive shoulders in a shrug. "Nothing."

The murmuring around the room resumed.

"If you won't hurt me, will you allow me to look for them?" Zac asked.

"Well," said the monster, "they are probably not here. We would know if they are home; we can sense them."

Zac had Valeria's wand stashed in his pocket. He removed it, still amazed by its appearance. He remembered back in the synagogue how the thought of light on the tip of the wand caused it actually to happen. He, therefore, conceptualized a big fire in his mind—closing his eyes for a minute and pointing the wand downwards.

Suddenly, a massive flame appeared, so large that it immediately consumed everything in its wake, including the large table in the middle of the room and also the lead monster.

The large fire caught the monsters completely off-guard, and they were all thrown off their feet as a sudden massive blast of hot air changed the aura of the room. There were loud and desperate screams as Death visited them like an unpleasant dinner guest. The barking ghosts were also yelping in horror as they struggled to get out of the place.

At World's End

Zac's coat caught fire, and he dropped the wand to the ground, immediately getting consumed by the flames and burning with loud, crackling sounds like firecrackers.

Oh my God, Zac thought.

The fire spread rapidly and systematically, consuming several furniture items as well as monsters in its wake. The doors were already jammed with fleeing monsters, and the drapes had already caught fire in a spectacular flaming show.

The barking ghosts were howling so loudly that Zac had to plug his ears with his fingers momentarily. The living room was getting filled with a thick black smoke, and Zac started to cough desperately.

At World's End

Then, there was a loud deafening noise by the drapes, and it was accompanied by the shattering of the windows. Glass flew everywhere, adding a new hazard to the already murderous peril that had befallen anything that was breathing in the living room.

Zac saw his chance to escape, and he took it, jumping across the room past the simmering wood and the mutilated corpses, and hurling his body through the window. He landed with a hard thud on the open snow outside, immediately cringing at the sudden change in temperature.

The screams seemed to have only gotten louder with his face buried in the snow, and he quickly staggered to his feet, slipping and sliding on the icy ground.

At World's End

He immediately noticed that he had been surrounded by a dozen monsters, each of them staring down hard at him as he stood in the middle of their circle, helpless.

The last of the screams from the living room were subsiding, but entire sections of the small farmhouse were starting to collapse.

Zac knew that there was no place for him to run.

This was the end for him.

He closed his eyes and hoped that his death would not be painful or gruesome.

Chapter 24

At the moment that Zac was surrounded by the monsters, the snowfall let up for a moment, enough for four hooded figures to skirt through the darkness quickly, undetected.

As the fire brought down the beautiful farmhouse, injured monsters attempted to get away from the wreckage. There were monsters carrying their injured colleagues away from the inferno into the welcoming coldness of the snow.

However, there were unfortunate sufferers within the farmhouse itself who were directly victimized—either by the scorching flames or by the thick, black acrid smoke that was now rising to the sky in columns.

At World's End

The dark hooded figures did not reveal their presence, and they only moved from one group of monsters to the next, quickly like a flash of light. New screams rent the air as a new victim swiftly joined the fray.

The monsters that were closing in on Zac halted their approach towards the little boy, throwing their gazes around them as one monster after another fell to the ground with puncture injuries.

"What the hell is going on?" Asked one of the monsters with its thick, slobbering lips, allowing a gob of saliva to trickle down its chin. "Who are those people?"

They whizzed around the place, barely visible, their movements appearing like a blur.

At World's End

The other monsters turned their attention to the chaos that was developing before them, turning to the assailants and trying to attack the fast-moving hooded figures.

Amid the conflict, one of the hooded figures got right to Zac, lifting him sharply by wrenching his hand up and almost unbolting it out of its socket.

"Ouch!" Zac cried out, immediately realizing that it was a human hand that had pulled him up.

The other monsters were desperately trying to stop the zigzagging hooded figures. They barely took notice of the hooded figure that was supporting Zac to his feet. The other figures were moving so quickly through the snow that they were living copious trail marks.

"Grandpa?" Zac said, astonished when he realized the identity of the hooded figure helping him to his feet.

The person removed the hood that was covering his entire head, revealing the aging face of Grandpa. He seemed to be particularly annoyed by the razing of his house, and he kept staring at it in disappointment.

The zigzagging hooded figures, now only three in number, had managed to kill almost all the monsters single-handedly, and Zac could not understand what was going on before him.

"How can you move like that?" He asked his Grandpa whose focus seemed to be on the

At World's End

disappointing scorched farmhouse before them. It had been reduced to a dark, simmering rubble, and there was barely any evidence to suggest that it was once a beautiful home.

The screams around them had subsided, and the monsters in the snow who happened to be still alive were waving their hands desperately in the air. The hooded figures stopped crisscrossing all over the snow, and the area looked like an ugly wreckage.

There were ugly, green dead bodies everywhere, and the snow had been enriched with a mixture of different colors, from red to black to blue. There was a decaying odor in the air combined with the strong smell of the voluminous smoke.

At World's End

"Come with us," said Grandpa, grabbing Zac by the shoulder and pointing in the general direction of the synagogue.

"I came looking for you, Grandpa," said Zac, "in the synagogue. Were you amongst the hooded people in there?"

The other hooded figures had gotten alongside Zac and Grandpa. They retained their hoods, and they started at Zac through the darkness that was their faces.

One of the last monsters to have died shouted defiantly in their direction; "Don't believe them at all, they are the murderers, Zac. Believe the truth for yourself, boy."

At World's End

One of the hooded figures proceeded through the snow to the monster to drive a dagger so deep in its chest it came out on the back side and gushed a rich red elixir of blood into the snow.

Zac was glad to be back with his grandfather because now, he would have the opportunity to ask him to help him get out of the South Pole. Taking into consideration that their house was already torched to the ground, Zac felt that he would meet no opposition with a proposition to leave the South Pole.

For good.

No way was he coming back to a weird place such as this.

At World's End

He could not get the death of Valeria out of his head. None of what was happening made any sense to him, at all.

His Grandpa started pulling him across the snow, away from the house. Zac was not worried about where they would spend the night because it was his intention to get transported out of this weird place immediately. He did not want to spend a moment longer in the place.

"Grandpa," said Zac, "Can you get me out of this place?"

Grandpa did not respond. They were walking rapidly through the snow, the sounds of the collapsing embers of what was once the farmhouse behind them being slowly replaced by the crunching of their footsteps as they moved across the snow.

"Is it possible, Grandpa?" Zac asked again, this time leveling a glance at his grandfather.

Grandpa stared at Zac, and that was when he noticed that Grandpa's eyes were of a particularly dark color, with his eyeballs suddenly growing bigger.

They stopped walking for a moment as Grandpa suddenly fell to the ground clutching his chest and crying out.

"Hey," said Zac, his shoulder feeling a sense of relief as Grandpa's grip on it disappeared.

At World's End

Grandpa sunk his face into the snow, writhing in pain. Zac sunk right beside him.

"What's wrong, Grandpa?"

Zac looked up for assistance from the other hooded figures but was surprised to see them walking on through the snow in the direction of the synagogue. They ignored what was happening.

"Hey! Come back!" Zac shouted at them, but it seemed inconsequential.

When he looked at his grandfather, suddenly wondering what he was going to do, he noticed it.

The familiar thick, black spines.

Like those of a porcupine.

At World's End

Growing right out of his chest.

"N-no, no," Zac stammered to himself, failing to believe what he was seeing before him.

The spines grew fast and rapidly, spreading all over Grandpa's body. He lay there silently, writhing in pain, the only sounds were the sickening sound of a sharp item piercing flesh.

As Zac watched in horror, he got to his feet, unable to kneel next to whatever was transforming before him.

Grandpa's body disappeared and was gradually replaced by a large, black phoenix bird with sharp claws, but with shut eyelids.

At World's End

All around its body on the snow, there was a black residue, like ash, sprinkled on the snow.

And then its eyes opened very abruptly, and the creature lunged off the snow and went straight for Zac's face.

Chapter 25

A strong wind was blowing, and it rifled Zac's black hair on his head. Consequently, his vision came to, and he realized that he was seated on a grassy section of the peak of a hill.

Behind him, there was strange, looming darkness, and Zac could not see anything beyond the blackness.

He blinked once as if to ensure that his eyes were working properly, and then he slowly got to his feet, wiping his hands on his stained jeans.

He felt his blood coursing through his veins very quickly, and it inspired him to imagine that the worst was behind him. There was the gracious sound of the gentle breeze and birds chirping overhead.

At World's End

The sky was a mixture of asymmetrical blue and white lines, with a very small cloud cover allowing the sun in the distance to penetrate its rays all the way to Zac's face.

It was a truly beautiful place to be, and he felt a strange sense of calmness being in a place where he could smell the distinct odor of flowers in the spring.

Then, his seemingly heavenly outlook of everything was suddenly shattered when he realized that there was somebody – or *something* – that had been keeping their eyes on him the entire time.

There was an elf standing in front of him, staring at him with its deep, engorged eyes and its skin on its face floppy and overlapping downwards. The elf wore

At World's End

an ugly grey rug that clung onto its bony shoulders

desperately, and its long, sharp yellow toenails

matched impeccably with its inexcusable teeth.

Zac was unsure where the elf had unexpectedly

appeared from—it seemed to have morphed right out

of thin air.

"W-who are you?" Zac stammered.

The elf bowed gracefully and majestically, answering:

"I'm Grelda, the messenger."

Zac shrugged.

"I have been sent here to show you everything," said

the elf, its small, disproportional body being suddenly

consumed by Zac's shadow as he came close to it.

At World's End

"Cause me no harm," it said in a croaky, bullfrog voice, raising its hands over its ugly head.

Zac stared closer at the elf, eyeing its strange body.

He had never seen one before.

"What do you want to show me?" Zac asked.

The elf gestured with its head.

"Come. I'll show you everything."

Zac did not understand, but followed the elf a short distance as it bubbled over to the edge of the hill where they beheld a scenic view before them.

At World's End

Zac could see the whole world from where he was standing, and he stopped paying attention to the elf and marveled at the beautiful sight before him.

They were standing atop a grassy hill on the Land of Ice, and before them, the Earth stretched endlessly, encircling a massive patch of ice at the center of the universe. Zac could see Atlantis from where he was standing—the small island in the middle of the Atlantic bordered by the African continent and the Americas continents on either side of its eastern and western peripheries.

Zac could also see the sun revolving slowly and purposely above the earth, categorically washing one section of the world in dull, yellow light while the opposite side had a thin, white light emanating from the moon in the darkened section of the Earth.

Zac could see that entire landmasses were covered in green, and the air seemed to be owned exclusively by the birds. He could also see the wild animals roaming freely, and there seemed to be a strange sense of peace about the place such that it made Zac feel nervous.

The landforms were particularly beautiful, with Zac taking note of beautiful valleys and breath-taking stretches of woodland. There were mountains everywhere, capped by snow and numerous streams of water cascading through the lands with larger water masses situated arbitrarily throughout the landmasses.

At World's End

"Watch closely," said the elf in a quiet, husky tone.

Then, Zac started to see a strange sight on the very peripheries of the earth—the oddest creatures that he was yet to see.

At first, he thought he had seen a beautiful woman, gliding through the air aided by wings that seemed to be strapped on her back. She was a beautiful black woman, with dark hair cascading from her head all the way to her back, and she had a smile that seemed infectious.

Her eyes were blazingly beautiful, and even though she was a significant distance away from where Zac and the elf were standing, Zac could not imagine anybody he had ever seen who was half as beautiful as she was.

And then he realized it—much to his shock.

"Hey," said Zac, turning to the elf, "are those wings actually part of her body?"

The elf did not say anything but nodded.

Zac watched as she landed gracefully on the very edge of the world to the north-west. He did nothing to conceal his surprise as he observed the same movement from three other similar creatures as they glided through the mushy clouds to the four edges of the world, each of them taking up position, and their wings flapping together on their backs like hands clasped in prayer.

At World's End

The four creatures maintained their positions on the edges of the world, watching over the wildlife and the beautiful landforms below them.

Then, strange darkness seemed to steal over the land and swept through the sun-lit and moon-lit landmasses, causing a strange coldness to emanate onto the place.

The angels abruptly stood upright, their wings on their backs spreading out grandly, making their bodies look much bigger than they actually were. They were clutching large flaming swords in both their hands. Zac felt a strange sensation in his body, that familiar tingly feeling that usually warned him of impending danger.

At World's End

And then, flying quietly and undetectably, the sky was snappishly filled with large, black, ugly flying monsters, with long, blade-like wings and reptilian eyes. They resembled the birds of the sky, except that they were almost different in every way.

Zac realized that they were coming from behind them—from the cold, impending darkness that seemed to be surrounding the dominant parts of the world.

The four beautiful winged creatures on the edges of the world started to attack the large, flying beasts with humongous blades. They swung their swords at the beasts, but they seemed to have no effect.

At World's End

The flying monsters grouped together, their scaly skins gleaming off the rays of the sun. They roared loudly at the winged creatures, their fiery red eyes locking onto their opponents.

The winged creatures seemed to have resigned to their fate—each of them was completely surrounded by at least a dozen monsters, and there was no way they were going to take them on successfully.

The flying monsters raised their heads simultaneously, and to Zac's shock, the animals proceeded to exhale fire from their opened, scaly mouths.

Zac could barely hear the screams of the winged creatures as they were immediately consumed by the flames and turned to smoldering remains.

Chapter 26

All the four corners of the world were gushing with thick red blood despite the fact that the winged creatures were burned to death. The blood soaked up into the ground, transforming the edges of the earth into thick, impenetrable ice barriers.

The ice just formed in an instant, and it spread so fast, rushing and encroaching the Earth at top speed and making such a frightening sound as it approached Zac that he cried out in panic.

"We should get out of here," he said to the elf, but the elf did not move. Instead, he replied:

"Be calm, master."

At World's End

The slain winged creatures suddenly appeared in the sky for a moment, formed in the shape of the clouds. They stared down at Zac and the elf with big, relieved smiles on their faces.

The moving ice finally got to the spot where Zac and the elf were standing, encroaching from both sides. The moving ice from the opposing sides collided right in front of Zac, and he winced, raising his arms to his face and preparing for the inevitable pain.

But there was nothing.

When he opened his eyes, the land that he was standing on that was once covered with beautiful greenery had now been replaced by an ice-covered ground. The hill that they were standing on had now been turned into a block of ice, and there was some light steam rising into the sunny atmosphere.

Zac noticed that the sudden ice transformation had no effect on the monsters that were now roaming the skies of the world nor the wild animals roaming freely in the landmasses.

The mass of ice had effectively enclosed the earth, acting as a boundary. The ice wall went so high up— right to the point where Zac and the elf were standing, and it appeared high enough to prevent even the flying monsters from leaving the center of the universe.

"What the hell is this?" Zac asked.

"Watch and see," said the elf.

At World's End

Zac felt frustrated. He grabbed the excuse-of-a-cloth the elf was wearing and threw him to the ground. He pinned the elf with his knee, suddenly noticing how cold the icy ground was.

The elf cried out.

"Where the hell am I?" Zac asked.

"Master," said the elf, raising its hands to protect its face and trying to keep as much of its body off the ice as possible. "Cause no harm to me."

"Then, tell me," said Zac.

"You are witnessing the birth of the world, master," said the elf in a frightened voice. "Cause no harm to me."

At World's End

Zac let go of the elf's rug apparel and got to his feet. The large monsters were still patrolling the skies.

"What are those?" Zac asked.

The elf got to its feet, brushing off the coldness of the ice on its side.

"Those are magical creatures, master," said the elf. "They are dragons."

"Who sent them?"

"The first human beings, master," said the elf. "To make the world free."

Zac frowned. "Free?"

The elf nodded. "Yes, free."

At World's End

Zac watched as the scene before him changed, but it took a significant period for it to display a different scene. The dragons eventually lost their ability to fly, falling to the Earth and disappearing into the rubble.

Then, Zac watched and saw that there was a thriving human community on one specific landmass—Atlantis. Then, it progressively disappeared under the water and never reappeared again.

The people who were once living on Atlantis spread out to the rest of the world—different families traveling to the farthest sections of the world and establishing homes and villages in those places. These new families found a way of living peacefully with the wildlife that was more dominant on the Earth.

At World's End

Then, a small, secretive group of people emerged from the rest of the families—a group of people that was unconventional in every way, from the way they dressed, the way they spoke and communicated to the way they behaved.

Despite being spread out to every corner of the world, this group of secretive people frequently met, forming enigmatic ways of control that resulted in conflicts that pushed the dispersed families closer to each other.

This secretive group of people proceeded to take control of every resource that the families acquired to survive. They created the first currency—mineral gold, and they would not reveal to the rest of humanity the true origin of the currency until after several centuries of working on its true origin, from

mining.

The secretive group of people was also responsible

for the changing landscape of the world, as a steady

encroachment of constructions would eventually

result in the formation of cities across the Earth to a

point where there were so many human beings that

Zac could not even fathom to count.

"What is all—" Zac started to ask, but when he looked

down, the elf had disappeared. Puzzled, he looked

around him, but all the could see was the endless ice

that was starting to make the whole place ice-cold.

Then, it started snowing.

At World's End

When Zac looked up into the sky, he noticed that all he could see was darkness.

When he looked around him, it progressively dawned on him that he was no longer atop the hill, but he was, in fact, in a very lonely place that he could not fathom.

The blackness around him seemed to be alive, almost elated, dancing in different shades all around him.

Zac watched in surprise as the darkness started casting its authority nearer and nearer to him, closing in on his very being.

What's going on? Zac asked himself.

At World's End

The darkness continued to dance around Zac, edging closer and closer to him with every movement.

Zac watched as the darkness finally enveloped him tightly, coiling around him in a bizarre embrace like that of a snake.

He felt death closing in on him. He could almost taste it on his tongue, the vile tastelessness of its delicious assurance. He knew that he would be at peace with himself very soon.

He closed his eyes for what he hoped was the final time.

Chapter 27

An old angel with a thick white beard that matched his apparels got to his feet and stretched out his exhausted hands. There was a big smile on his face, and it did reveal his surprisingly white and well-kept teeth.

"How did you like that story?" He asked.

There was a younger angel seated in front of his desk in his expansive office.

The young angel took a moment before he could reply. He had been inside the office for the past few hours, but he was still completely taken in by the scenery that was surrounding them.

At World's End

The walls of the office were made of pure glass, and this meant that the young angel could see through to the regal forest beneath them and to a distant sea near the horizon.

There was light streaming everywhere. It was so much that it made the white-bearded old man one with the light. The young angel did find his voice, though:

"That was an interesting story," he said. "I still don't get it."

"What don't you get?" The old angel asked.

"The boy," said the young angel, "the main character in your story. Zac, was it?"

"Yes," said the old angel. "What about him?"

At World's End

The young angel shrugged a little. "Well, first of all, I don't get why he is important—I haven't understood why he's so different from everybody around him, but more importantly, what happens to him?"

The old angel laughed a little. He shuffled to the far end of the room where there was a glass table with an array of bottles, clutched his sides, then poured himself a rich red drink into a small glass.

"I don't k-know," he said in between gulps.

"Didn't you write the story?" The young angel asked.

"Yes," replied the old angel, pouring himself another drink.

At World's End

"Then, let me just give you a basic piece of advice," said the young angel.

"Says the inexperienced writer who's only aspiring and has nothing to his name," retorted the old angel.

"Regardless of what you might think of me," said the young angel, "the story would be much better if you just kill off the main human. It is important that you show our people these humans for the vile scum they actually are."

The old man was preoccupied with his drink at that moment.

"The small human boy should be killed off—confirm it at the end of the story."

At World's End

The old angel shrugged.

"I intend for life to follow that course," said the old angel, "I have already put it in print. The human boy, just like the elf, is a messenger."

"But I just think that the work can never be a masterpiece," said the young angel, now getting to his feet and walking slowly towards the door.

The old man set his glass down on the table.

"Wait," he shouted.

The young angel stopped in his tracks, right at the door.

"Why is it not a masterpiece?" The old angel asked.

At World's End

"Because you have revealed too much," said the young angel. "The humans must never know. A good story is one that doesn't inform them."

The old angel had a puzzled look on his face.

"A true magician never reveals his secrets," the young angel said with a smile.

He let himself out, closing the door behind him.

fin

Connect with us on our Facebook page
www.facebook.com/bluesourceandfriends and stay
tuned to our latest book promotions and free
giveaways.